Ben nodded. "Okay then. I'll be back a little before six. See you then."

She thanked him again and scooted out of the truck. He watched her bounce up the walk, swinging her purse. She paused on the porch, turned around, waved, and then disappeared inside.

Ben sat at the curb for a few minutes, drinking in the ostentation of the brick and mortar two-story house. He'd been in too much of a rush this morning to really look at it, but at close examination, it was incredible. Pillars extended from the bricked porch floor to the second-story roof. At least three chimneys stretched toward the sky. The garage behind it could easily hold four vehicles. He craned his neck, his eyes widening. Was that a pool house?

He shook his head, curiosity overflowing. A huge house, servants, the silver rocket. . . Why was someone who obviously had no need to work filling a minimum-wage position at New Beginnings? There was more to Angela Fisher than met the eye. Suddenly Ben was determined to get to the bottom of her secrets. Maybe this evening would help shed a little light on things. . . .

KIM VOGEL SAWYER, a Kansas resident, is a wife, mother, grandmother, teacher, writer, speaker, and lover of cats and chocolate. From the time she was a very little girl, she knew she wanted to be a writer, and seeing her words in print is the culmination of a lifelong dream. Kim relishes her time with family and friends, and stays active in her church by teaching adult Sunday school, singing in the choir, and being a "ding-a-ling" (playing in the bell choir). In her spare time, she enjoys drama, quilting, and calligraphy. She welcomes visitors to her Web site at www.KimVogelSawyer.com.

Books by Kim Vogel Sawyer

Heartsong Presents
HP693—Dear John
HP709—That Wilder Boy

Promising Angela

Kim Vogel Sawyer

Heartsong Presents

For my critique partners, past (Beverly, Jill, and Darlene) and present (Eileen, Margie, Ramona, Staci, Crystal, and Donna).

Thank you for your consistent mentoring.

And with a special hug to Eileen. You know why.

A note from the Author:
I love to hear from my readers! You may correspond with me by writing:

Kim Vogel Sawyer
Author Relations
PO Box 721
Uhrichsville, OH 44683

ISBN 978-1-59789-276-6

PROMISING ANGELA

Scripture taken from the HOLY BIBLE, NEW INTERNATIONAL VERSION®. NIV®. Copyright © 1973, 1978, 1984 by International Bible Society. Used by permission of Zondervan Publishing House. All rights reserved.

All of the characters and events in this book are fictitious. Any resemblance to actual persons, living or dead, or to actual events is purely coincidental.

Our mission is to publish and distribute inspirational products offering exceptional value and biblical encouragement to the masses.

PRINTED IN THE U.S.A.

one

Angela Fisher hugged her counselor, waved good-bye to the receptionist, wrapped her fingers around the handle on her suitcase, and walked out the door to freedom. When she'd entered the South Central Drug Rehabilitation Center eight weeks ago, she had a chip on her shoulder the size of Mount Gibraltar and an attitude to match. Today, the only weight she carried was that of her well-filled suitcase. She smiled. It felt good to have those burdens lifted.

Squinting against the mid-July sun, she turned toward the bus station. When she'd called her parents to let them know she'd be free to come home, she'd hoped Mom or Dad would volunteer to drive over and get her. But Dad had a charity golf game, and Mom gave the excuse of a meeting with the library board about hosting a multicultural exhibit.

"Can't you take a bus home, darling? I know you have money for a ticket," her mother had purred. And Angela had consented. Angela didn't fault her parents for their community involvement, but it had rankled a bit that a golf game to raise money for a piece of sculpture to stand in the center of the city's newest roundabout and a planning meeting took precedence over their daughter's release from an intensive drug-abuse rehabilitation program.

Of course, Angela acknowledged as she waited at the curb for the WALK sign, seeing the center would be a reminder to her parents that she hadn't been away at summer camp or something equally innocuous. Their embarrassment at her being ordered to go through the rehabilitation program was beyond description.

Angela stepped off the curb and followed the crosswalk, the leather soles of her sandals slapping the asphalt a little harder than was necessary as she contemplated the real reason for her parents' shame. She suspected it had more to do with her getting caught, and the subsequent publicity, than it did with her need for the program.

But more than one good thing had come as a result of her time at the center. Not only had Angela confronted the reason why she'd chosen to use drugs and made the decision to avoid them in the future, she'd also discovered a relationship with Jesus. A friend from back in Petersburg, Carrie Wilder, had visited. She'd brought Angela a Bible and shared the message of salvation. Maybe it was loneliness that first made Angela listen to Carrie, but recognition of her need for a Savior brought about the decision to accept Jesus into her heart.

Her steps lightened. She was going home a new person—drug free and Spirit filled. That thought brought a lift to her heart, and she almost skipped as she made her way down the sunny sidewalk.

Weaving between other Saturday-morning pedestrians, she flashed a smile and offered an "excuse me" when her suitcase bumped the leg of a middle-aged woman. Despite her effort to be polite, the woman snapped, "Watch what you're doing!"

Angela spun around, a sharp retort forming on her tongue. Before she could spout the words, lessons from the Bible Carrie had given her winged through her mind, dispelling the unpleasant rejoinder. With a meek smile, Angela said, "I'm terribly sorry," turned, and hurried on.

She sucked in a big breath of the dry summer air and offered a silent *thank You* to the Holy Spirit for controlling her errant tongue. Angela knew she would need the help of the Holy Spirit in the next weeks—and not just in keeping her tongue under control. In her final one-on-one session, her counselor had cautioned her the first weeks back "in the world" would be the most challenging.

"Habits are hard to break," the woman had warned, her expression serious. "Here, in a safe environment, it's easy to stay drug free. But back in your community, back with your old friends, the desire to be a part of that lifestyle will be a fierce pull. It will take a great deal of strength to resist the temptation."

At the time, Angela had released a laugh and said blithely, "Oh, don't worry about me! I'm as headstrong as they come. Nobody can make me do something I don't want to do." And then she'd added, "Besides, I have Someone helping me stay clean. I won't go back to those habits."

The near argument with the grumpy lady on the sidewalk had seemed to be a small test of the Holy Spirit's hold on her heart, and it pleased Angela that she'd passed with flying colors. Now if she could continue doing the right thing when it was bigger than making a cutting retort. . .

"Angela!"

The call pulled Angela from her introspection. She swung around, her hand shielding her eyes from the glaring sun, and sought the source of the voice. She broke into a smile when she saw Carrie Wilder trotting down the sidewalk. The moment Carrie caught up, she wrapped Angela in a huge hug.

Angela laughed in Carrie's ear, releasing her suitcase to return the hug. "Carrie! What are you doing here? Did you come to visit? I got out today."

"I know." Carrie slipped her sunglasses to the top of her head, the earpieces acting as a headband for her long blond waves. "I wanted to give you a ride home."

"Oh, Carrie!" Angela grabbed her friend in another hug. "That's so sweet of you! You drove three hours over here just for me?"

Carrie's light laugh brushed aside Angela's concern. "Well, why not? It's a great day for a drive."

"Oh, this is wonderful. Thank you!" Angela picked up her suitcase and admitted, "I was dreading that bus ride."

"Well, I parked at the center, so now we have to walk back there. I've been chasing you for two blocks—you walk fast!"

Angela laughed and looped her elbow through Carrie's. "Yes, I suppose I'm eager to get home."

"I don't blame you," Carrie said. They ambled easily down the sidewalk, no longer in a need to rush since they didn't have to follow the bus schedule. "I imagine it's been a long eight weeks."

Angela puckered her lips into a brief, thoughtful pout. "Yes, it has, but it's been a good eight weeks. I learned a lot—about myself and about why I felt the need to use drugs in the first place. And I hope I've learned how to keep from giving in to that need in the future. I don't want to have to come back."

Carrie sent her a worried look. "Do you really think that might happen?"

Angela shrugged. "My counselor told me it isn't uncommon. But I'm determined to beat the odds. Besides"—she smiled, giving Carrie's elbow a squeeze—"thanks to you, I'm not fighting this battle alone. One of the verses you underlined in the Bible you gave me says, 'I can do everything through him who gives me strength.' I'm going to bank on that."

Carrie slung an arm around Angela's shoulders and gave her a one-armed hug. "Good for you!" Releasing Angela, she stepped off the curb and popped the trunk on her sports sedan. "Let's get you home and put those words into action."

They pulled through a fast-food place and ordered burgers, fries, and shakes before catching Highway 54 East and heading for Petersburg. Angela took a long pull on the straw, savoring the sweet chocolate flavor of her milk shake. The food at the Center had been filling but bland. She sighed, tipping her face to smile at Carrie's profile.

"I'm going to have to be careful. Food tastes so good right now. I'm afraid I'll overindulge and outgrow my wardrobe."

Carrie laughed and popped a crispy french fry into her mouth. "I wouldn't worry too much about that. You'll be too busy to be snacking."

Angela put her shake in the cup holder as worry struck. "Do you know what I'll be doing?" When she'd been arrested for drug use, the judge had handed down a one-year sentence, starting with the eight-week rehabilitation program. There were still ten months to be served somewhere. It was at least a small comfort to know someone who worked in the county clerk's office. Hearing the details of her sentencing might be less painful coming from a friend.

One hand on the wheel and her gaze on the road, Carrie reached into the backseat and groped around. It took a minute before she brought her hand forward and dropped a large manila envelope in Angela's lap. "The judge's recommendation is in there."

Angela peeled the envelope open and pulled out a sheaf of stapled pages while Carrie continued.

"Basically, it says since this is a first offense, you will serve your term with community service. He's assigned you to work at New Beginnings, starting this coming Monday."

"Monday already. . ." Right around the corner. Then Angela's hands froze on the papers as a wave of fear rose up inside her. "New Beginnings? You mean, the place Rocky's brother runs, where they train handicapped people for jobs in the community?"

Carrie nodded, a soft smile appearing on her face with the mention of her husband's name. "The very same. I suggested it to Philip, he thought it was a great idea, and the judge approved it."

"But—but—" Angela shook her head. "I don't know anything about working with people with disabilities!"

"You'll learn."

Carrie's nonchalant comment set Angela's teeth on edge. "You don't understand, Carrie. I wish you'd asked me before you talked to Philip." Angela shifted sideways in the seat to face her friend. Her mouth felt dry, and she took another quick slurp of melting milk shake to moisten her tongue. "People with handicaps. . .they make me nervous."

Carrie flicked a brief glance in Angela's direction. "How so?"

Angela thumped the shake back into the cup holder. "I don't know. They just do! I've hardly visited my aunt Eileen since she took that job as resident caretaker for those three men at Elmwood Towers. Every time I'm around them, I get. . .nervous. I don't know how to talk to them, how to be around them. . ."

"You'll learn."

Angela clutched the hair at her temples. "Stop saying that!"

"Why? It's true." Carrie munched another fry, unconcerned.

"The more you're with them, the easier it will get."

Angela flopped back in the seat, her eyes closed. "I'm not so sure about that. . . ." Her stomach churned. New Beginnings! She would never have imagined being sent there. . . .

"Well, it's either community service at New Beginnings or a women's detention facility. I was pretty certain you'd prefer New Beginnings."

Angela opened her eyes. She drew in a big breath then released it slowly, forcing her tense shoulders to relax. When it came to choosing between glorified jail or working with adults with disabilities, it was pretty much a no-brainer. Of course she preferred the latter. It was just. . .awkward.

"Listen"—Carrie's soft voice held a hint of sympathy—"what was that verse you were telling me about before we got in the car? 'I can do everything. . .'"

" 'Through him who gives me strength.' " Angela sighed, shaking her head. "Okay, okay, Carrie, you got me. New Beginnings it is." Shooting her friend a sharp look, she added, "But don't expect me to be good at it. I know nothing about working with people with disabilities."

Carrie chuckled. "You'll learn."

⁂

Ben Atchison placed the clipboard on his desk, crossed his arms, and scowled across the room. That new hire, Angela Fisher, was backing off from Danielle when she should be moving closer. He shook his head. What had Philip Wilder been thinking when he brought that girl on staff?

If Philip weren't happily married, Ben would have suspected the boss just intended to add to the décor. That little turquoise and black number she had on today fit her to perfection, showcasing every trim curve. How she managed to stay upright—not to mention look graceful—in those skinny-toed, back-half-missing, toothpick-heeled shoes was nothing short of miraculous.

And her hair! Ben had never seen anything like it—reddish-brown spirals that bounced across her shoulders and caught the light with every movement. The first time he'd seen those curls, he'd been tempted to catch one and pull it to see how far it would stretch. But of course he had kept his hands to himself. She also had the most unique eyes—pale blue with a deep gray-blue rim around the irises. A man could get caught up staring into those eyes and lose track of time without any effort at all.

He drummed his fingers on the clipboard, the *thp-thp-thp* underscoring his thoughts. Yep, that Angela was one gorgeous woman. But she obviously had no desire to work here. The tight smile, wringing hands, and stiff posture gave her away. So why was she here? He snorted. It sure wasn't for the paycheck. He didn't think she needed it, based on the high-class outfits she'd worn each day this week. Plus, he'd seen what she drove to work—the sleek silver rocket had brought a neck-popping double take and an appreciative whistle from his lips. She obviously had a source of income from somewhere that exceeded anyone's salary here at New Beginnings.

So again. . .why was a woman like that working here?

Across the room, Danielle, her round face shining, opened her arms for a hug. Ben watched, holding his breath, waiting for Angela's response. Although they worked with the clients to teach them the appropriate time and place for hugs, affirmation was needed and freely given in appropriate ways. If Angela rebuffed Danielle, refusing to acknowledge the other woman's silent plea for approval, he'd have some choice words to share at the end of the day.

Angela tipped her body backward away from Danielle, extended her arm, and patted the other woman's back in a stiff, impersonal manner. Her face twisted in a grimace. Ben frowned, wondering if that grimace was an expression of dislike or discomfort. He did understand that sometimes people had difficulty relating to those with handicaps, and the discomfort could display itself in dislike when it was truly just insecurity.

Danielle giggled, covering her mouth with both hands and hunching up in pleasure. She patted Angela's shoulder, then reached once more for the broom and dustpan. The two women went to another area of the work floor to practice more. *Thp-thp. . .* Ben's fingers drummed. Dislike or discomfort? He couldn't be sure when it came to Angela.

But it was his job to make sure the clients were treated with respect and dignity. No hired worker—not even one with such a pleasing appearance—would be allowed to destroy the fragile confidence of his clients. He'd keep an eye on this new hire—Angela Fisher. A few more days—just a few more days to give her a chance to settle in. If he didn't see improvement, he'd visit with Philip, and his recommendation would be to let Angela Fisher go.

two

Angela uncapped her pen and drew a big X over the last Friday square on the calendar that hung inside her work locker. Two weeks down. . . How many to go? With a rueful chuckle, she decided not to count.

She closed her locker, leaned her forehead against the cold metal, and sighed. Tiredness smacked her, but it was a good kind of tired, she realized. The tired that comes from working hard and giving of yourself. In spite of the tight knot between her shoulder blades, satisfaction filled her. All that praying to get through the days must be helping.

Pushing off from the locker, she turned and gave a start. Ben Atchison, seated at his desk, had his gaze aimed right at her. Without conscious thought, she flipped her head to tousle her curls then ran her fingers from forehead to crown, teasing the curls into an uneven side part. It was a gesture she'd used to good effect many times in the past when she'd wanted to capture a man's attention.

She'd noticed Ben watching her quite a lot since she started at New Beginnings. And to be honest, she didn't mind. Ben was a hunk deluxe. Broad-shouldered. Trim-hipped. With bulging biceps that told of time in a gym.

He could let his hair grow, though. It was short enough to qualify for the military. So short it was hard to determine its true color—maybe blond, maybe brown, maybe brownish blond. But she didn't have to guess at his eye color. Those piercing eyes of deep blue, hooded by thick, arched brows, were like beacons in his square, chiseled face.

Oh yes, Ben Atchison was a very pleasant package. She allowed a smile to curve her lips, tipping her head and meeting his gaze directly so he'd know the smile was meant for him. Then, realizing what she was doing, she spun to face her locker, her cheeks blazing with heat. She shouldn't be flirting. It was a habit she struggled to break, along with so many other habits she knew didn't please her Savior. And flirting with one of the bosses was certainly a huge mistake. Opening her locker, she hid behind the door to get a grip on her embarrassment.

Her gaze fell on the Bible resting on the top shelf. She lifted it out. She had formed the routine of reading during her afternoon break, and she wanted to continue the schedule at home over the weekend. Bible in hand, she closed the locker with a snap and turned to leave. And she yelped in surprise. Ben Atchison stood beside the lockers, his blue-eyed gaze pinned on her face. They hadn't been in such close proximity since her first day when he'd shown her the time log and assigned her a locker. Up close those eyes were like magnets, drawing her in. She gulped.

He didn't smile, and his deep voice sounded very formal. "Angela."

Clutching her Bible to her chest, she croaked, "Yes?"

Ben folded his arms, his weight on one hip. "I just wanted to let you know I have your two-week evaluation completed. I plan to show it to Philip this evening, and then you'll receive a copy on Monday. If you agree with my assessment of your performance, you'll simply sign off, and we'll have a second evaluation at six weeks. If you have any areas of disagreement, you, Philip, and I will schedule a conference to discuss it."

Angela managed a nod. So that's why he'd been watching. She suddenly felt very foolish. "I—I'm sure your assessment will be fair." Dropping her gaze to the floor, she confessed, "I know I'm not very good at this, but I am trying."

"I know. I can tell."

Her chin shot up, her startled gaze bouncing to meet his once more. He'd sounded. . .nice.

He pointed to the Bible she continued to hug like a lifeline. "I noticed you reading during breaks. What book are you studying?"

Angela glanced at the Bible in her arms. A light, self-conscious laugh escaped. "I'm not sure you'd call what I'm doing studying. The Bible is kind of new to me, so I've just been skipping around, reading here and there." Realizing how flighty that sounded, she hastened to add, "But I'm enjoying it, and a lot of it is really making sense."

Ben tipped his head, his brows coming down. "Are you a Christian?"

"Yes, I am," Angela said. "But I'm afraid I'm as new to Christianity as I am to New Beginnings. I have a lot to learn in both areas."

His nod seemed to hold approval. "What church do you attend?"

Angela blinked. "Church? Well, I don't—I just got back from"—she swallowed, seeking words that would be honest yet would protect her—"a training program, and I became a Christian while I was away. I haven't found a church yet."

"Your family doesn't attend?"

Angela stifled the laugh that threatened. Her parents? In church? Her mother gave up that "gobbledygook," as she called it, when she graduated from high school, and her father had never been interested. They did attend the big church downtown for Easter and Christmas services, but that was more for public appearances than anything else. If Petersburg didn't have a huge, statued, bricked, bell-towered church, her parents probably wouldn't bother at all, but Dad felt walking into that ostentatious building gave him some prestige.

She realized Ben still waited for an answer. She shook her head. "Uh-uh. My parents aren't churchgoers."

"Well, I attend a small church out on the highway. It's called Grace Fellowship. The building used to be a restaurant, but it closed years ago. I know it isn't fancy"—his gaze swept up and down her outfit, creating a rush of embarrassment— "but we have a growing young adult group, with services on Sunday morning and evening, as well as a Wednesday night Bible study. Would you be interested in attending?"

Her heart skipped a beat at the thought of being in a formal study group. Carrie had encouraged her to join a church where she could grow. "Oh, yes, I'd like that a lot!"

His warm smile made her tummy tremble. "Good. Would you like to attend this coming Sunday morning? I'd be glad to give you a ride."

Fluttering her lashes, Angela quipped, "It's a date."

Immediately she regretted her action. How easily she'd slipped into flirtation. Again. But it wasn't appropriate—not for this setting and with this situation. The warmth in Ben's eyes disappeared to be replaced with a guarded look that was like a splash of cold water over Angela.

"I—I mean I would very much appreciate a ride. Thank you." Her stuttered words did little to ease the tense moment.

Ben gave a brusque nod. "What's your address?"

At least he was still willing to take her. Her hands shook as she penned her address on a scrap of paper and handed it over. She offered a meek smile. "Thank you again, Ben. I do appreciate the ride."

He looked at the address, and his eyebrows shot upward. She knew what he was thinking—everyone in town was familiar with the Eastbrook Estates. She waited for him to change his mind and tell her she wouldn't fit in at his simple, used-to-be-a-restaurant church, but he slipped the paper into his breast pocket and said, "I'll be by around nine fifteen. Sunday school starts at nine thirty, and the worship service at ten forty-five."

"That's fine. I'll be ready. Well. . ." She waved a hand toward the door, inching in the direction of the exit. "I told my aunt I'd stop by after work and have some milk and cookies with her." A nervous giggle erupted. Had she really just told Ben she'd be having milk and cookies?

But he didn't make any snide remarks. He didn't even smirk. With a quick upturning of lips, he turned toward his desk. "I'll see you Sunday morning. Have a good weekend."

"Yes. . .Sunday. And thank you." Before she could say or do anything else to embarrass herself, she escaped.

&

Ben curled the fingers of one hand around the steering wheel as he maneuvered through the late afternoon traffic toward Elmwood Towers. His other hand tapped restlessly on the fold-down console. A pepperoni pizza sat in the passenger seat, its aroma teasing Ben's senses. He tried to focus on his upcoming dinner with his cousin Kent to get his mind off of the mouthwatering spicy smell—and off of Angela Fisher.

Why had he invited her to church? Or more specifically,

why had he offered to take her? She had transportation—he whistled—boy, did she have transportation! Yet he'd opened his mouth and offered her a ride in his six-year-old midsized truck that didn't even have a backseat to put some distance between them. He gave the console a pat. At least the twelve-inch barrier would be in place.

If he didn't want to get close to her, why had he issued the invite? He knew why. There had been something in her unusual light blue eyes. . . . When she'd admitted she had a lot to learn both as a New Beginnings employee and as a Christian, a little something inside of him had melted. The insecurity lurking in her eyes had been all too familiar. He understood the feeling. Empathized with it. A dozen years ago he had felt lost and uncertain, and a schoolmate had reached out to him. What a difference it had made.

He didn't know how he would have managed the past few years without the strength of Christ bolstering him. The loss of his father and uncle in a boating accident, followed by Kent's spiral into drug addiction, were burdens that would have overwhelmed him had it not been for his reliance on Jesus. Ben's heart ached at the route Kent had taken to find comfort. He sensed in Angela the same longing for acceptance and peace.

As Angela's direct supervisor, it was his responsibility to mentor her at work. As a Christian, it was his responsibility to be a good example. Inviting her to church was one way of mentoring.

Mentoring. . . That was it. Just mentoring. . .

A red light brought him to a halt. His thoughts skipped backward, replaying the flutter of her eyelashes and the flirtatious, "It's a date." His fingers curled over the edge of the console. He hoped he'd managed to squelch that idea. In his observations over the past two weeks, he'd surmised Angela had lived a rather self-serving lifestyle. She was entirely too flippant, too self-absorbed. If he were going to date, he'd want someone warm and soft, with an aura of holiness brought through a relationship with Jesus.

Not to mention someone who didn't shy away from the disabled. Shaking his head, he replayed several recent scenes. Yes, as he'd told her, he knew she was making an effort, but she had a long way to go to be completely accepting and supportive of the clients at New Beginnings. Anyone he dated would eventually be around Kent, and he wouldn't risk having Kent hurt by someone's withdrawal.

The light changed, and he pulled forward, a small niggle of guilt striking at his thoughts. He hoped he wasn't being judgmental. But Angela, despite her physical beauty, didn't possess the qualities he wanted in a life mate. It would be unkind and dishonest to lead her to believe he had any interest in her beyond employer to employee, Christian mentor to mentee. He'd have to watch himself, not give her the wrong idea.

He turned onto Elmwood Avenue, the last stretch. The six high-rise apartments of Elmwood Towers loomed ahead. Kent waited in Tower Three. Ben whispered a quick prayer of gratitude for the assisted-living apartments in each of those towers. It had taken some fancy footwork by New Beginnings' owner Philip Wilder to get one quad in each of the retirement village's apartment buildings designated for adults with handicaps, but what a service it was to those in the community who faced challenges.

Getting Kent into one of those apartments had done him

so much good. The small measure of independence had boosted Kent's confidence, built his self-esteem, and put him more on a level with his peers. What single man in his late twenties wanted to live at home with his mother?

Ben pulled into a visitor's space, shut off the ignition, and picked up the pizza box. Hitting the automatic lock on his key chain, he turned toward Tower Three, but a glint of silver caught his eye. He stopped, turned, and stared.

Sure enough. The silver rocket—Angela's car—sat six stalls over.

three

Angela popped the last bite of her fourth chocolate chip cookie into her mouth, swigged the final gulp from her half-pint carton of milk, and released a satisfied sigh. "Oh, Aunt Eileen, that was wonderful." She patted her stomach, laughing. "But I think I'd better skip supper tonight! I'm going to waddle out of here!"

Eileen and her friend Alma, on the couch facing Angela across the low walnut table scattered with magazines, empty milk cartons, and cookie crumbs, both laughed. The older women exchanged winks.

"Now, Angela, when you look like me"—Eileen gave her own bulky midsection a two-handed squeeze—"you can worry about waddling. Until then, neither of us wants to hear about it!"

All three women laughed. When Angela arrived at her aunt's apartment after work, Eileen had suggested taking the cookies to the foyer of Tower Three and sharing with a friend of hers who'd been down in the dumps since a hospital stay. At first Angela had balked, not willing to share Aunt Eileen with anyone else. But seeing Alma's enjoyment of the cookies and conversation made her regret her selfishness. She had a lot to learn about reaching out to others, she realized.

Aunt Eileen would be a great teacher in that regard. Her mother's older sister was unpretentious, warmhearted, and open, unlike the rest of Angela's family. Eileen and Angela's mother had grown up dirt-poor, but while Mother had sought riches in married life, Eileen had married a salesman who made little more than enough to pay the necessary bills. Uncle Stan had passed away years ago, leaving Eileen alone, yet she had never wallowed in self-pity. Angela held great admiration for her aunt, even though her parents often commented with a hint of disdain that their lifestyles didn't "mesh."

The smell of pizza wafted through the foyer, and Angela looked over her shoulder toward the double doors. She did a double take when she saw who carried the pizza. She leaped to her feet. "Ben?"

"Ben?" Eileen repeated, shooting Angela a smirky grin.

Angela felt her face flood with heat. How disconcerting to have him walk in after having spent a good fifteen minutes entertaining the two older ladies by describing his physical attributes and being teased about his Sunday invitation.

He glanced in her direction and imitated her double take, coming to an abrupt halt that nearly sent the pizza flying from his palm. Grabbing the box with both hands, he took two steps in her direction. A wary smile creased his face. "Angela. . .hi. I didn't expect to see you here."

Angela brushed cookie crumbs from her lap. She hoped she didn't have any crumbs on her face. "Ben, I'd like you to meet my aunt, Eileen Cassidy, and her friend Alma. . . ?" To her embarrassment, she couldn't remember Alma's last name.

But Ben smiled. "Hello again, Mrs. Andrews. It's good to see you home and looking well. Kent told me you had quite a time. And Mrs. Cassidy, nice to see you, too. Philip was just mentioning he needed to come by here and see what you're up to."

Angela swung her gaze back and forth, listening, her jaw

hanging open. Eileen knew Ben?

Eileen laughed as she pushed to her feet, her eyes twinkling. "Oh, that Philip. He couldn't take better care of me if he were my own son."

Ben's warm smile sent Angela's heart pattering even though it was aimed at Eileen. "I know he thinks the world of you." He paused, rocking on his heels, then took a hesitant step toward the elevators. "Well. . .I'd better go. Pizza's getting cold, and I'm expected."

"Bye, Ben!" Eileen called, waving a pudgy hand.

Alma added, "Have fun with Kent!"

The moment the elevator doors closed on Ben, Angela wheeled on her aunt. "Aunt Eileen! Why didn't you tell me you knew Ben?"

Eileen sat back down, shrugging. She wore a look of innocence. "How was I to know the Ben you were talking about is the same Ben I know? There are a lot of Bens in the world." Her sparkling eyes gave her away even before the giggled snort blasted out. "Of course I knew you were talking about Ben Atchison. What other Ben works at New Beginnings? He's a wonderful young man, and I'm tickled pink you two have formed a friendship."

Angela collapsed against the back of the couch. "I'd hardly call what we have a friendship. . .yet." Her heart gave a hopeful flutter. "But—" She leaned forward, suddenly eager. "Tell me everything you know. Who is he meeting here? This Kent—is he an uncle?"

Alma shook her head, her wrinkled face sad. "No, honey, not an uncle. His cousin. A young man not much older than you."

Angela shook her head as understanding dawned. These apartments housed retirement-age individuals except for those few apartments set aside for the special-needs community. Then that meant. . . She bit down on her lower lip as she glanced toward the elevator doors. Turning back to Alma, she said, "You mean his cousin is handicapped?"

"I'm afraid so." Alma pursed her lips, her face creasing in disapproval. "The result of a drug overdose. He'd been perfectly healthy up to that time." She shook her head, her chins quivering. "Such a waste. . ."

Angela swallowed. The cookies suddenly didn't set so well. "So—so what's wrong with Kent? What did the overdose do?"

Alma sighed. "Such a tragedy. . ." She leaned forward, licking her lips.

Eileen patted Alma's hand. "We should be careful not to gossip."

Alma's cheeks mottled with pink. "Oh, well, I certainly wouldn't want to do that. . . ." She reached for another cookie.

Angela felt a little twinge of guilt for encouraging gossip. She'd indulged in more than her fair share of unnecessary talk over the years. But small wonder—Mother was so good at it. However, that wasn't an excuse. Another habit she needed to break. She winged a silent prayer for God to keep her aimed in the right direction; then she returned her thoughts to Ben.

Her heart ached as things fell into place. Kent must be why Ben worked at New Beginnings. He had a personal stake in reaching out to those with disabilities. Something else struck hard, making her heart race. Kent's disability was the result of drug use. *That could have been me. . . . Oh, thank You, Lord, that I didn't go that far. . . .*

She stood again, forcing a smile to her lips. "Aunt Eileen, thank you for the cookies. And, Alma, I'm so glad I got to meet you."

Alma nodded. "Oh, me, too, dear. You come see me again, will you?"

Angela took the wrinkled hand in her own. The loneliness in the old woman's eyes pierced her heart. "Of course I will." Who would have imagined Angela Fisher making a promise like that to an old lady? Yet she vowed to carry through on the promise.

Eileen rose and embraced Angela. Cupping her face in her sturdy hands, she whispered, "Now you take good care. I'll be praying for you."

Tears flooded Angela's eyes. Aunt Eileen must be thinking the same thing she had earlier—how fortunate it was that she had escaped with little more than a one-year sentence of community service for her drug abuse. Poor Kent served a lifetime sentence. . . .

"Thank you," she said, smiling. "I'll take those prayers."

As she headed for her car, her thoughts drifted to one of the apartments where Ben sat eating pizza with his cousin. How sad. How very sad. . . She reached into her purse for her keys, and her fingers brushed against something sharp. She withdrew the item—a small, folded square of paper.

A chill struck. She knew what it was. A phone number. For Gary. Dropping her purse, she tore the paper into bits of confetti and scattered them in the gutter. She didn't need that number. She didn't want that number.

But what frightened her was the desire that welled up when she'd remembered what calling that number could gain.

She clenched her fists and vowed aloud, "I'm not doing that anymore!" She snatched up her purse from its spot on the ground at her feet, slammed herself into her car, and zoomed for home as if demons were chasing her.

❧

Ben pushed a napkin into Kent's fist and teased, "Use that thing, man. You're making a mess."

Kent threw back his head and laughed. He raised the napkin to his face and swished it back and forth in a jerky, awkward movement. When he dropped his hand to his lap, the pepperoni grease had been cleared from his lips and mustache. A bit still shone in the chin whiskers of his beard, but Ben knew he'd get it cleaned up in his shower.

"Good stuff, huh?" Ben asked as he took another bite.

"Ye–es, good. . ." Kent's face contorted as he formed the words. He patted his stomach. "Full."

Again, Ben resorted to teasing, a throwback to their junior high days when zinging one another was a sign of affection. "No kidding! You ate three-fourths of that thing by yourself."

Kent's laughter lifted Ben's heart. As boys, growing up, they'd been more like brothers than cousins. They'd played on the same Little League team, been members of the same scout troop, and rarely spent a Friday night without a sleepover. They'd had pillow fights and arguments over girls and quizzed each other for spelling tests. Best friends—inseparable. Until the accident that claimed both of their fathers' lives. After that, things had changed.

Ben swallowed his pizza, a lump in his throat making it difficult. If only Kent had known the Lord, he would have sought comfort in prayer rather than in drugs. Ben understood why Kent had turned to alcohol and drug use. The pain of losing a father was a pain too heavy to bear without help. Kent had found his "help" in the most hurtful way available. And it couldn't be changed now. Ben just had to pray that somehow God would use Kent's disability for someone's good.

He leaned forward and tapped Kent's bony knee. "Hey, want to go down to the workout room?"

Kent's eyes lit up. "Go. . .pump iron."

Ben nodded. "Yep. Let me throw this stuff away." He reached for the empty pizza box and crumpled napkins.

"No!" The word burst out, anger twisting Kent's face. "My apartment. I. . .clean up."

Ben raised his hands in surrender, a smart-alecky grin on his face. "Yes, sir! You clean up, sir!" He did his best private-to-sergeant imitation.

The anger faded as quickly as it had flared. Kent laughed. Calm again, he said, "You cook. . .I clean up."

Ben remained seated on the edge of the sofa as Kent gathered the napkins and stacked them in the pizza box. He battled to close the lid, and Ben grabbed his own knees to keep from helping. Ben knew Kent needed to exercise every bit of independence. No matter how hard it was to watch his cousin struggle, he wouldn't interfere.

Finally, after a few frustrated grunts, Kent managed to get the lid closed, trapping the napkins inside. With a triumphant grin, he placed the box in his lap then wheeled his chair to the kitchenette and dropped the box into the waste can.

Spinning around, he crowed, "Ready. . .to pump. . .iron!"

"Got your key?"

Kent patted his jeans pocket.

"Then let's go." Ben opened the apartment door and waited until Kent rolled through before giving it a slam. He poked Kent on the shoulder. "Wanna race?"

Kent's determined scowl reminded Ben of when they were twelve and Ben had issued a challenge. Ben knew Kent remembered little of those days—the overdose had stolen the majority of his memory—but Ben remembered. He knew Kent would lean forward, stick the tip of his tongue out between his lips, and squint at the finish line—in this case, the elevator doors.

"Okay," Ben said, getting into position with a hand on his knee. "Ready, get set. . .and go!"

Ben could have won easily, but he deliberately stayed one pace behind the wheelchair. Kent's raucous hoot of satisfaction was all the reward he needed.

"Awwww!" Ben feigned disgust, slapping his thigh. "You got me again."

Kent pointed at him with both index fingers, his face creased in a huge smile. "I got you. . . . I got you. . . ."

Ben thumped his cousin's shoulder. "Way to go, man." He poked the elevator down button then crossed his arms, pretending to mope. "Well, I'll get you in the workout room. You won't lift more weight than me."

With sparkling eyes, Kent shook his head and raised his fists as if showcasing his muscles. "I will. . .beat you."

The elevator doors slid open. Ben gave Kent's wheelchair a push. "We'll just see about that." As they rode toward the lobby, suddenly Ben wondered about Angela. Would she still be down there? He hoped not. If she looked at Kent the way she looked at the clients of New Beginnings, Ben was fearful of how he would react.

four

"Amen."

Angela added her voice to the others who echoed the close of the final prayer. The naturalness of the act gave her a feeling of warmth and acceptance she wanted to savor. Lifting her face to meet Ben's gaze, she smiled.

"I really enjoyed the service, Ben. You were right—this is a great church."

Ben's shoulders lifted in a shrug, shifting his tie. He smoothed it back into place as he said, "The Holy Spirit is here. You can sense it."

"Yes, you can." Angela allowed her gaze to sweep around the room, observing the small groups of chatting congregants. Despite the simplicity of the block building and the essence of grease that lingered in the air, no one seemed in a rush to leave. All appeared at home and comfortable in the makeshift sanctuary.

And although several people had welcomed her this morning with smiles and handshakes, no one had startled at her name. No one pointed or whispered, as she had feared. She couldn't deny being relieved about that. Even though Carrie had prompted her to join a church immediately upon her return from rehab, she had hesitated out of worry. If people recognized her, they might steer clear of her based on her past mistakes. The humiliation of her arrest still hung like a chain around her neck. Being reminded of it by people's reactions added another link to the chain.

But no one had left her feeling uncomfortable this morning. She felt at ease and eager to be a part of the church family. Turning a slow circle, she sought faces from Sunday school, trying to recall names. She hoped the opportunity for friendship existed among the singles her age. Her drug-abuse counselor had encouraged her to form new friendships with people who were not a part of the "partying" scene. She would be more likely to remain clean if she stayed away from users. Of course she had Carrie, but she didn't want to rely on Carrie too much. As a newlywed, Carrie needed her time with Rocky. And Angela needed to broaden her horizons.

"Are you ready to go?" Ben looked down at her, a soft smile in his eyes.

She liked his Sunday face—contented, open. Sometimes at work she got the feeling he didn't quite trust her. Her heart raced as she realized how much less he would trust her if he knew about her past. Even though she knew total honesty was important in any relationship, she still hoped he'd never find out. The open friendliness would surely whisk away, and she wasn't sure how she would handle that.

They slipped from between the rows of folding chairs that served in place of wooden pews and ambled toward the foyer area, which would have been where the cash register sat when the building served as a restaurant. "I really liked the focus verse from this morning," Angela commented then frowned, pressing her memory. "What was the reference?" She stopped and consulted the printed program an usher had offered when she'd come in.

"Ephesians 1:4," Ben said. A grin twitched his cheek as he watched her open her Bible and search for Ephesians. "Here."

He took the Bible, opened it to the right place, and then handed it back.

"Thanks." Angela grimaced. "I guess I need to get some of those little tab things with the names of the books to guide me."

"No, don't do that." Ben shook his head. "You'll always use the tabs then and never learn to find them for yourself. Try memorizing the order of the books instead."

"Oh, okay. I'll try that." Lowering her gaze to the open Bible, she slid her finger to verse four and read aloud. " 'For he chose us in him before the creation of the world to be holy and blameless in his sight.' " With a sigh, she closed the Bible and hugged it to her chest. "I never really thought about His creating us to be holy before Him."

Ben smiled. "Well, we are created in His image, after all. Sin messes that up though. That's why God sent His Son, Jesus, to die for our sins. It is through His sacrifice that we can be cleansed from all unrighteousness. He makes us holy once again."

Angela blinked at him, awed by his knowledge. "Wow—you've been a Christian a long time, haven't you?"

Ben smiled. "A few years."

"Oh, I hope I'm as smart as you someday!"

He released a light laugh. "Well, Angela, one thing you'll find out." He put his hand on her back to guide her toward the door. "No matter where you are in your Christian journey, there's still a lot to learn."

Angela nodded. Carrie had said pretty much the same thing. That's why it was important to attend church, for the opportunity to continually grow. They left the air-conditioned building and walked across the balmy parking lot to Ben's truck. "I have a lot to learn in many areas, I'm afraid," she said.

He opened the door for her. "What areas?"

Angela climbed in then waited for him to settle behind the steering wheel before answering his question. "Well, for instance, you. . . I was so surprised to see you at Elmwood Towers yesterday after work. I didn't know you had a cousin who lived there."

Ben shot her a sharp look. "How did you know I was visiting my cousin?"

Angela waved good-bye to a couple of people as the truck pulled out of the parking lot. She looked back at Ben. "My aunt—Eileen Cassidy, remember? She told me your cousin lives there."

Ben nodded, his lips set in a grim line. Then he took a deep breath, and his expression cleared. "I really like your aunt. She's a spunky lady with a big heart. On which side of the family is she related?"

Rebuffed, Angela explained her family tree, but beneath her words her thoughts raced. *Why did Ben change the subject when I asked about his cousin? Could it be he's shamed by what his cousin did?* Her heart twisted painfully in her chest. If he could be ashamed of his very own cousin, he would certainly feel even more animosity toward a stranger. She carefully guarded her words as Ben drove the familiar streets toward her family's estate.

It was best that Ben never found out that she had been arrested for drug use.

❧

Ben battled guilt as he listened to Angela, her voice halting at times, share about her relationship with Eileen Cassidy. He hadn't switched gears out of anger, but he suspected by her quiet demeanor she felt as though he were angry. Protectiveness toward Kent welled up again.

Kent had suffered so much rejection since the drug overdose. His own mother and sister had little to do with him, furious at him for wasting his life. His friends had all abandoned him. What good was he to them, trapped in a wheelchair, unable to join them in their parties? Even strangers on the street shied away from him. Ben knew how much those rejections hurt Kent, and he wouldn't willingly put Kent in the line of fire for more pain.

Angela's discomfort around the clients at New Beginnings made it clear how she'd react to Kent—and Kent wasn't stupid. He recognized when people avoided him. Despite his other handicaps, he was still fully capable of feeling. The less Angela knew about Kent, the better. Ben would not give her the opportunity to hurt his cousin.

He stopped the truck along the curb and shifted into park. He looked at Angela, and the yearning he'd seen in her eyes last Friday, right before he invited her to church, was there again. It took him back, and he found himself opening his mouth and blurting out a second invitation.

"Did you catch the announcement about the potluck dinner before the evening service? If you'd like, I can swing by and pick you up."

Angela's gaze shot to her lap. She clenched her fingers on her Bible. "Potluck. . . That means everybody brings food, right?"

Ben chuckled. "Well, yeah. Then we all share it."

She took a deep breath, her gaze still down. "I'd probably better not, then."

What was bothering her now? Determined to make up for his earlier evasiveness, he assumed a teasing tone. "Why? Don't you eat?"

She turned her face slightly to look at him. Worry and

uncertainty showed in her eyes. "I—I can't bring anything."

He could make no sense of that comment. "Why not?"

A huge breath huffed out, and she flipped her hands outward. "I can't cook!"

Ben burst out laughing. "You're kidding, right?"

She glared at him.

His laughter died. "You really can't cook? But—you're what—twenty-one, twenty-two?"

"Twenty-three," she said grimly. "And I know how pathetic it is, but. . ." She paused, biting down on her lower lip for a moment. Finally she sighed and admitted, "Ben, I never had to do much of anything in the way of chores while growing up. We've always had servants. Mother said menial chores were beneath us, and Dad insisted that's what he paid the maid and cook to do. So, I just haven't learned."

Ben stared in amazement. Her comments sure explained a lot about her standoffish behavior at work. But never having chores was beyond the scope of his understanding. He and his sister had been responsible for household duties from an early age. Especially after Dad died, Mom had depended on them to help out. And now that he was grown, he appreciated it. He lived alone, but he could take care of himself, cleaning house, doing laundry, cooking—and not just dumping soup from a can—real cooking.

"Well. . ." He scratched his head. "I tell you what. I'll bring the covered dish and you just. . .come."

Her jaw dropped. "You can cook?"

He managed to swallow his laughter. "Yeah. I make a mean enchilada casserole with chilies and onions and lots of gooey cheese. Sound good?" He was amazed how important it had become to put her at ease.

Her lips quivered into a weak smile. "It does sound good, but. . ." She tipped her head, her curls spilling across her shoulder and catching the afternoon sun. "Are you sure it's okay to go and not bring anything?"

He grabbed the steering wheel with both hands before one sneaked out and captured one of those spiraling curls. "Perfectly okay. So. . .do you want to go?"

A full smile lit her face. "Yes, I do. Thank you."

Ben nodded. "Okay then. I'll be back a little before six. See you then."

She thanked him again and scooted out of the truck. He watched her bounce up the walk, swinging her purse. She paused on the porch, turned around, waved, and then disappeared inside.

Ben sat at the curb for a few minutes, drinking in the ostentation of the brick and mortar two-story house. He'd been in too much of a rush this morning to really look at it, but at close examination, it was incredible. Pillars extended from the bricked porch floor to the second-story roof. At least three chimneys stretched toward the sky. The garage behind it could easily hold four vehicles. He craned his neck, his eyes widening. Was that a pool house?

He shook his head, curiosity overflowing. A huge house, servants, the silver rocket. . . Why was someone who obviously had no need to work filling a minimum-wage position at New Beginnings? There was more to Angela Fisher than met the eye. Suddenly Ben was determined to get to the bottom of her secrets. Maybe this evening would help shed a little light on things. . . .

five

Angela glanced up from the dishwashing station when she heard the tinkle of the bell announce a visitor. She looked toward the door, and an involuntary gasp accompanied the tensing of her body. The visitor was hers—Officer Brighton. He held a brown paper bag at his side. Angela's heart flip-flopped in her chest.

"Angela? Are the cups done?"

Angela, flustered, turned back to Steve. The man pointed to the cups stacked in the dishwashing tray. She gave a quick glance at the cups lined up in the plastic tray and pushed her lips into a smile.

"You did a great job, Steve. You filled all the slots. Now can you check to be sure all of the cups are upside down? Remember, we don't want them to fill up with water."

Steve beamed. "I will check."

"Thanks." She gave his back a pat, her gaze on the officer who remained just inside the door, scanning the room. A movement to her left captured her attention—Ben leaving his desk to welcome the visitor. Angela began inching away from the dishwashing area. "Steve, you check those cups; then you can start on the silverware, okay?"

"Okay, Angela!"

Angela paused long enough to make sure Steve would follow her directions, and then she darted across the room and cut in front of Ben, bringing him to halt. She offered what she hoped was a natural smile. "It's okay, Ben; it's for me. I'll get it."

Ben scowled briefly, glancing at the officer, but he nodded and returned to his desk.

Angela hurried to Officer Brighton. Weaving her fingers together, she pressed her hands against her jumping stomach. "Hello. I didn't expect to see you here."

The man glanced at his wristwatch, his face impassive. "The records we have indicate you are entitled to a midafternoon break. Is this not the case?"

"Yes, I do have a midafternoon break, so I could be free for a few minutes." Angela shot a nervous look over her shoulder. Sure enough, Ben was watching.

"Very well, then." He lifted the paper bag. "Take this, and—"

Angela slipped her hand through the officer's elbow to interrupt him. "Come with me." She guided him to the break area where tall partitions shielded them from view.

He frowned and pulled loose the moment they rounded the corner. "Miss Fisher, I—"

"I know why you're here." Angela blinked rapidly as nervousness churned her middle. She lowered her voice to whisper. "It's the random drug test, right?"

He nodded. Holding out the bag again, he boomed, "If you will just—"

Angela whammed her finger against her lips. "Shhh!" She darted to the partition and peeked out. Everyone appeared busy except Ben, who peered in the direction of the partitions with a puzzled frown on his face. She zipped back to the officer.

"Officer Brighton, the only person who knows I'm here on community service is the owner. I—I don't want the others to know. Especially—" She stopped herself before she blurted out Ben's name. *Why is it so important for him not to know?* Her heart pattered. She knew why. His friendship had become very important to her in the short amount of time she'd known him. She didn't want him to be disappointed in her.

She clasped her hands beneath her chin and gave her best pleading look. "Please, can't we do this later? I promise I won't leave work. You can pick me up and take me wherever you need to get the test, but I just can't do this here."

"Miss Fisher, the purpose of a random test is—"

"I know, I know, to catch me off guard, which you've certainly done." A nervous giggle burst out, which she muffled by clapping her hand over her mouth. When she felt she had control, she leaned toward the officer and lowered her voice to a rasping, fervent whisper. "But I won't be any less off guard at five thirty. Oh, please, don't make me do this here!"

"Miss Fisher, I'm sure you understand there are procedures we follow to be certain the test is accurate. If I leave now, after having notified you that you will be tested today, the results can be skewed."

Angela wasn't completely sure she understood everything he'd said, but his meaning came through. He didn't trust her. She felt her cheeks fill with heat, humiliation striking. But then why should he trust her? She'd used an illegal substance. She deserved his suspicion. But it didn't make it any easier to bear. God may have forgiven her, but men. . . ?

Lifting her chin, Angela met the man's gaze. "Officer Brighton, I know I made a huge mistake. I'm sorry for it. At the time, I wasn't a Christian, and I didn't much care if I did wrong things. But now I have Jesus in my heart, and I don't want Him to be disappointed in me. I'm not perfect, but I'm trying very hard to do what's right." She swallowed. "You don't have any reason to believe me, but I'm being honest when I tell you I won't do anything to make the test skewed. Please let me do this after work."

The officer stood for a long time, his face set in a firm scowl, looking directly into her eyes. Angela held her breath, waiting for him to make his decision. Her thoughts begged, *Please, please, please. . . !*

Finally Officer Brighton released a sigh. "Very well, Miss Fisher. I will return at five thirty and escort you to the police station."

Angela thought her legs might collapse; the relief was so great. "Oh, thank you!"

"But make sure you're here and ready to go." He moved toward the gap between partitions, but before exiting he turned back. "You'd better be honest with me. The judge will not take kindly to fraudulence."

Angela wondered briefly how one could be fraudulent with a drug test, but she didn't ask in case he thought she wanted the information for future reference. Instead, she gave a brisk nod, meeting his gaze with an earnest look. "I understand. And I promise"—she held up her fingers, Boy Scout-style— "no fraudulence."

He gave her one more sharp look before striding out of the break area and heading for the door. She followed on his heels, a smile plastered to her face, her gaze on the back of his shirt. She felt as though everyone in the room was watching her, but she refused to glance around and confirm the feeling.

At the door, she chirped in a loud, cheerful voice, "Good-bye now! Thanks for stopping by! I'll see you later!"

The look on his face communicated clearly he thought she'd

lost her mind. But he didn't say anything. He just stepped out the door.

Angela pressed her forehead to the closed door for a moment, bringing her erratic breathing under control. And when she turned, her gaze collided with Ben's. Immediately her heart kicked into double-time. She straightened her shoulders, flashed a smile, and wiggled her fingers at him in a ridiculous semblance of a wave. Then, with a deliberately bouncy step, she headed to the dishwashing area to check on Steve.

Ben's gaze nearly bore a hole through her back.

⊷

Ben checked the hourly schedule for the clients at the recycling center for the third time, and it still didn't make sense. Not because the schedule was wrong, but because his focus was somewhere else. He pushed the schedule aside and released a huff of annoyance. Rarely did he have trouble staying on task at work even though his desk sat in the middle of the various centers, surrounded by activity and voices. So why today?

His gaze found Angela at the corner table with three other clients, instructing them in the skill of wrapping cloth napkins around silverware. The fluorescent lights glinting off her curls gave her an angelic appearance. A smile yearned for release, but he swallowed it. Another jolt of—something—struck him, and he forced his gaze to the desktop, his thoughts churning.

He had fought the urge all afternoon to corner Angela and ask about the man who had visited. As her supervisor, he had a right—technically speaking. Visitors were frowned upon during working hours. But, in her favor, she had used that brief visit as her afternoon break and had worked through the scheduled break, so he couldn't accuse her of taking advantage.

Still, who was the man? Her familiarity with him was obvious, the way she'd taken his arm and escorted him to a private area. The giggle he'd heard had created a knot in his gut. Angela hadn't mentioned a boyfriend. He shook his head. What difference did it make if she had a boyfriend? Was he jealous?

That question brought his gaze up to connect with hers once more. He'd made a determination to mentor Angela both at work and in her Christianity. It wasn't supposed to go deeper. Yet, somehow, in the course of seeing her every day at work and sitting with her in church, she'd managed to weasel into his heart.

He jerked backward, his chair springs complaining with the sudden movement, and shifted his gaze to the ceiling. *Lord, You're going to have to direct me here. Angela is a Christian, and I do find her attractive, but there are a lot of differences between us. What is Your will concerning our relationship?*

He didn't receive an instant answer to his simple prayer, but that didn't bother him. He'd learned over the years that God had His own timing. Ben could wait for his answer because he knew eventually it would come and it would be best for him. The bell hanging above the front door sent out its tinkling ring, bringing Ben from his chair. The bus driver for Steve and Doris had arrived.

He spent the next thirty minutes seeing clients out the door, bestowing hugs and high fives, and visiting with parents and caretakers about the progress being made by clients. This was one of Ben's favorite parts of his job—seeing a mother's face light up with pride in her adult child's accomplishments as she realized the child would be able to take a job, earn a wage, and function like any other contributing member of society. Ben loved his work, the opportunity to serve and bring positive changes into people's lives, and he felt the curiosity about Angela's mysterious visitor melt away as he went through the end-of-day routine.

But when the last client had gone, and the employees were filtering out the door, Ben walked to the break area to retrieve his refillable soda cup and found Angela at the table, head low, shoulders slumped. Her dejected pose brought an immediate rush of concern.

Sliding into the seat beside her, he touched her arm. "Angela? You okay?"

She glanced at him. Tears glinted in the corners of her pale eyes, bringing out the deeper ring of blue gray around the irises. She shrugged. "Not really, but. . .I will be."

"Something happen with one of the clients? I can help you with that."

A shake of her head brought shimmering motion to her hair. "No. Nothing like that. The clients are great. I think we're learning to work well together."

Ben nodded. He agreed. He had seen subtle changes in Angela's behavior around the clients. She still had a ways to go to be completely at ease, but she wasn't shying away from them now, and she didn't seem as stilted as she had the first few days. He processed her answer. If she wasn't upset about something with one of the clients, there were only two more options.

Either he or her visitor had upset her.

"Have I done something to upset you?"

Her head jerked up, her startled gaze meeting his head-on. "Oh, no! You've—you've been wonderful, Ben. So patient. . ."

But the tears plumped and spilled down her cheeks.

He fought the urge to push his fingers through her hair and draw her to his chest in a hug. She looked as though she could use the comfort. But a hug would be well beyond the bounds between employer and employee, mentor and mentee. He linked his fingers and rested his hands on the tabletop. "Then what is it?"

She seemed to search his face, creating a tightness in his chest. Her lips parted, as if ready to share, but then she clamped her jaw shut, shifted her gaze, and swept the tears away. "Nothing."

Ben forced a soft chuckle. "Now, I learned from growing up with a sister, females can be a little erratic with their emotions, but not even my sister cried over nothing. Are you sure there isn't something wrong?"

Angela kept her gaze aimed forward, giving him a view of her sweet profile. The curve of her jaw, framed by the tumbling curls, became more appealing by the minute.

"I just have to go somewhere—with someone—and I'm a little nervous," she finally said.

Her voice was so soft Ben had to strain to hear her. An image of the man who'd shown up earlier filled Ben's head. He curled his fingers around Angela's arm and gave a gentle squeeze. "The visitor from today, is that the 'someone' you mean?"

She still wouldn't look at him, but she nodded.

Ben felt something rise from his gut. Not quite anger, but certainly a strong emotion. "Has he threatened you in some way?"

Again her gaze spun in his direction. Her wide eyes expressed shock. "No! Nothing like that!" Then she lowered her gaze again, twisting her fingers together in her lap. "There's no threat at all. Don't worry."

Her flat words did little to assure Ben. Yet he could see she wasn't going to share anything more. He still held her arm, and he moved his hand to the back of her chair. Her curls brushed his fingers. "Angela, would you like me to pray for you?"

The tears returned, filling her eyes and bringing a luminance to the unusual irises. She nodded. "But I have to go." Shooting from the chair, she snatched up her purse and zipped around the partition. Moments later, Ben heard the bell tinkle and the door close.

He remained at the table, questions spinning through his head. He had no idea what had upset Angela, but he decided it really wasn't important that he know. God knew, and that was enough. He'd offered to pray, and he would follow through on it. Lowering his head, he closed his eyes and shared his concerns with his heavenly Father.

six

Angela rapped her knuckles against the door leading to Aunt Eileen's apartment and groused to herself. *Twenty-three years old and having to be babysat! It is beyond embarrassing.* Yet the judge's terms of her probation were firm: for the duration of her sentence, she must be monitored by a responsible adult or be placed in a detention facility.

With her parents' decision to take a month-long cruise, Angela needed someplace to go. Neither of her older sisters expressed enthusiasm about her joining them, but Aunt Eileen had cheerfully agreed to having a lengthy visit. At least, she conceded as she raised her hand to knock a second time, Aunt Eileen was fun. If she had to be babysat, Aunt Eileen was top choice as sitter.

The door swung open, and Aunt Eileen greeted Angela with a boisterous hug. "Come in! Come in!" She pulled Angela through the door and gave it a push to close it. "Sorry I didn't get here sooner. I was cleaning the shower."

Angela grinned. A towel was slung around Aunt Eileen's neck and a white smudge of some sort of cleaner decorated her left cheek. "You don't have to go to extra trouble for me."

Aunt Eileen waved a hand, shooing away Angela's words. "Nonsense! Old ladies clean. It's no extra trouble. Besides, I had to get all of Roscoe's hair out of there. He likes that rug in front of the sink for some reason." She chuckled and leaned down to scratch under the chin of the huge yellow and white cat at her feet.

"Well, okay then." Angela looked around the small living room. The apartment was so plain compared to her own home, yet she felt at ease here. Welcomed. She sighed, suddenly glad she'd come. "Where do you want me to put my stuff?"

Aunt Eileen took the suitcase from her hand. "In the second bedroom." She headed for the hallway, and Angela followed with Roscoe twisting around her ankles. Aunt Eileen continued. "I use it as a sewing room, but I borrowed a twin bed frame and mattress from someone at church. Nothing fancy, but it'll do in a pinch."

Angela stepped into the room. Aunt Eileen had draped the mattress with a multipatched quilt. The curtains were open, allowing in a shaft of sunlight, which highlighted the bright red and blue patches. She sat on the mattress and gave a little bounce while her gaze took in the sewing machine crunched in the corner beside a stack of plastic bins that overflowed with rolls of fabric and sewing notions. Something that appeared to be a half-finished quilt face lay across the end of the sewing machine table.

"Are you sure I won't be in your way in here? It looks like you're in the middle of something."

Aunt Eileen walked over and patted the bulky folds of fabric. "I am. But it'll keep. I can quilt anytime. But time with you? That's a precious commodity."

Mixed emotions mingled in her chest at her aunt's words. Not even her parents seemed to treasure time with her. She rose and gave Aunt Eileen another hug. "I love you, Aunt Eileen."

Aunt Eileen's chuckle sounded. "Aw, sweet girl, right back atcha. Now"—she set Angela aside—"I bet you've got more stuff to bring up, right?" Her eyes twinkled.

Angela laughed. How well Aunt Eileen knew her! "Well, a little, I guess."

Another chuckle let Angela know Aunt Eileen understood the meaning of "little" where any of Angela's family was concerned. "You can slide your empty suitcases under the bed, and I put some extra hangers in the closet for you. Sorry there's no dresser in here. Will that shelf do?"

Angela spotted the laminated, wood grain-printed shelf tucked at the foot of the bed. Spartan compared to her matching chest, mirrored dresser, and armoire in her bedroom at home. But she smiled and said, "Sure. It'll do fine."

Aunt Eileen crossed her arms, her brows coming down for a moment. "You'll have to go out to your car again anyway to get the rest of your things. Can I talk you into making a delivery on the way?"

"A delivery? Where?" Angela trailed Aunt Eileen to the kitchen where she withdrew a whipped topping container from the refrigerator.

Plunking the container into Angela's hands, she said, "Remember Alma? She hasn't been eating so well since she left the hospital. She says nothing tastes good. But she loves my pistachio pudding salad. I thought maybe this would entice her to eat."

Angela shook her head. "Aunt Eileen, why are you so nice and Mother is—?" She broke off, unwilling to insult her mother even if it was deserved.

Aunt Eileen smiled and gave Angela's hand a gentle pat. "Your mother is nice. She just has a different way of showing it."

Angela grimaced.

Aunt Eileen pulled her brows into a frown. "Think of all

the good she does in the community. All the committees she heads up and organizes. Aren't those nice things?"

"Well. . ." Angela shrugged. "I suppose they are. But somehow it's not the same as doing little things, like sending pistachio salad to someone who doesn't want to eat."

A chuckle sounded. "Those people who benefit from the fund-raisers probably wouldn't agree with you."

Angela chose not to argue. She headed for the door. "I'll take this over; then I'll be right back."

Aunt Eileen laughed. "Oh no, you won't! If Alma gets you in that apartment, you'll be there for a while."

Angela grinned.

"But don't worry about it. There's nothing in your trunk that will spoil, is there?"

"Of course not."

"Good." Aunt Eileen gave a brusque nod. "Then just enjoy the visit. Spread a little sunshine. It'll do you good." She ushered Angela out the door.

Forty minutes later Angela finally managed to work her way from Alma's kitchen to the front door. Her hand on the doorknob, she sent a big smile and offered a promise. "I'll be here a whole month. I'll come see you again, okay?"

Alma's face drooped. "Please do. I so seldom have visitors. . . ."

Angela followed an unfamiliar impulse and wrapped Alma in a warm hug. The spindly arms that clung back brought a rush of satisfaction through Angela's heart. It felt good to give. Really good. How she wished she'd learned that long ago.

Back in the hallway, she headed to the elevator, humming to herself. She pushed the down button, and within seconds the doors opened. Her tune ceased as her gaze fell on a young, bearded man in a wheelchair in the middle of the elevator.

"Oh!" She hesitated. "Is—is there room in there for me?"

The man grunted, but he pushed on the wheels of the chair, moving himself backward. Angela stepped past him to lean against the far wall. The doors slid shut, sealing them inside. The man's curious gaze fixed on her.

"Who. . .are you?" he asked. Although the words were somewhat garbled, Angela understood him.

She offered a smile. "I'm Angela."

"Why are. . .you. . .here?"

Her smile broadened. *Snoopy, isn't he?* "Oh, just visiting a friend."

"Who?" The word came out like a bark.

"Alma Andrews." Angela paused, tipping her head. "Do you know her?"

The slight nod gave his answer. The doors slid open, revealing the lobby. Angela gestured toward the opening, but he stuck out his jaw.

"Lad—ies first."

Angela's brows shot up in surprise. A snoop, but a gentleman nonetheless. With another smile, she edged past him then kept her hand on the door casing until he brought the wheelchair through. The man continued to eye her.

"You. . .go home. . .now?"

Angela wondered if he were trying to get rid of her. "No, actually I'm going to collect some things and head to my aunt's apartment. Eileen Cassidy. Do you know her, too?"

"Eileen is. . .my friend."

Somehow that didn't surprise Angela. "Well, then I'll probably see you again. I'm staying with Aunt Eileen for a while."

"Why?"

Angela decided that really was none of his business. But she smiled and said, "Just because." Standing beside his chair, she said, "Now I need to ask you a question. You know my name. What's yours?"

"K—ent."

"Kent. . ." Angela took an involuntary step backward. Ben's cousin. The one who suffered brain damage after a drug overdose. Sweat broke out all over her body. Swallowing, she forced her lips into another smile. "It's very nice to meet you."

He nodded. "I see you. . .later." Without another word, he caught the rubber of his wheels and gave a push, rolling in the direction of the lobby.

She stood for a long time, looking after him. Sympathy brought tears to her eyes. Despite the beard that covered the lower portion of his face and the dullness of his eyes, she could tell he was a handsome man. His arms showed evidence of strength, although his legs seemed thin beneath the loose denim of his jeans and his hands had appeared clumsy. To think he had been hale and healthy, and a foolish choice had wrought this permanent change.

Then another thought struck. Although initially uncertain, she had slipped into an easy conversation with him. Time with the clients at New Beginnings was obviously making a change in her heart. She hummed again as she headed for the outside doors. She hoped she'd see Kent again, and she'd be sure to give him a big hello when she did.

ટ

Ben balanced three boxes of Chinese takeout in one hand and pressed the handicap button with the other. Pizza last week, Chinese this week. Both were favorites of Kent's, so Ben alternated between the two, throwing in the occasional deli sandwich. The doors to Tower Three opened, inviting his entry, and he shifted the items into both hands as he passed through.

He headed toward the elevators, but a tinkling laugh caught his attention. Shifting his gaze to the lobby, he spotted the unmistakable curly auburn hair of Angela Fisher. And next to her, in his wheelchair, sat none other than his cousin Kent.

Kent sniffed the air. He shifted in his chair, searching, and his face broke into a huge smile. "Ben! My. . .friend!"

Ben moved on shaky legs toward the pair. "Hey, Kent." His gaze met Angela's. Her cheeks sported a pink blush. "Angela."

"Hi, Ben." She rose, her fingers linking in a now-familiar gesture of uncertainty. "I see you brought supper. Kent said you would."

Ben's gaze bounced between the pair. "Yeah. It's our Friday routine."

"That's what he said." With a light giggle, she added, "And here I thought you were this great cook. But you only bring Kent takeout." She nudged Kent's shoulder. "Is that because you're afraid he'll try to poison you?"

Kent's raucous laughter filled the room.

Uncertain how much longer his rubbery legs would hold him up, Ben moved to the sofa and leaned against the back. Angela. . .and Kent. . .chatting. Teasing. At ease. He'd been so afraid of letting her meet his cousin, yet it appeared they were very comfortable with one another. The wonder of the moment was more than Ben could comprehend.

She pointed to the cartons in his hands. "At least it looks like you brought something good."

"Chinese," Ben contributed, then felt like an idiot. Of course it's Chinese. What else would go into these little white boxes with the red squiggle on the side?

Angela's smile swung in Kent's direction. "What's your favorite Chinese food?"

"Beef. . .and broc. . .broc. . ." Kent made a horrible face then spat, "Broc'li!"

Angela laughed softly and gave Kent's arm a pat. "Wonderful choice. You get your protein and your vegetable that way."

Kent beamed while Ben stared in amazement. Angela— teasing with Kent. He hadn't realized how much she had changed in her brief weeks at New Beginnings.

"Well." Angela stepped around the sofa. "I'll go and let you two eat. I'll see you later, okay, Kent?"

Kent nodded his shaggy head, his eyes glowing. "I. . .see you later. . .An–ge–la."

"Bye, Ben." And she slipped out the door.

Ben stared after her, the cartons in his hands nearly forgotten.

"Ben."

Ben shook his head, trying to pull his scattered thoughts together. Angela was visiting with Kent like she'd visit with. . . anybody. He wished she'd stuck around a little longer and visited with him.

"Ben!"

The sharp note of frustration in his cousin's voice finally caught Ben's full attention. He turned to Kent. "Yeah?"

Kent pointed at the cartons. "I am. . .hun–gry."

"Yeah. Okay." Ben straightened and adjusted his hands for a better grip. Walking alongside Kent's wheelchair as they headed for the elevators, he said, "How long have you known Angela?"

Kent's shoulders raised in a brief shrug.

"But she's your friend, huh?"

Kent's smile turned knowing. "An–ge–la. . .is pretty."

Ben swallowed. "Yeah. . ."

"She is my. . .girl–friend."

Ben felt as though a rock fell from his chest to his stomach. Apparently Angela had been too at ease with Kent. Remembering times when he'd witnessed her flirtatious behavior, he wondered if she'd exercised some of that with Kent. If so, Kent wouldn't understand Angela was only playing.

He had a big problem on his hands, and it wasn't juggling Chinese food cartons.

seven

Ben awakened early Saturday with a headache. He knew he wasn't sick—unless it was sick with worry. Pictures of Angela with Kent had tormented his dreams, and he knew he wouldn't be able to rest until he'd settled the issue of Kent referring to Angela as his girlfriend.

He threw back his sheets and headed for the kitchen, planning his morning. She was staying at Elmwood Towers with her aunt. After breakfast he'd drive over and talk to her, make her understand she had to be careful where Kent was concerned. Sure, he wanted her to be relaxed and open around those with handicaps, but flirting with them was a completely different thing. The clients had to learn boundaries for behavior. Apparently Angela needed the same lesson.

He ate his scrambled eggs and toast as slowly as possible and extended his shower. No sense in arriving at the Cassidy apartment too early. Angela probably slept in on Saturday mornings. After the shower, he read the newspaper and even watched a few cartoons before deciding it was late enough to go.

Dressed in a pair of khaki shorts and a solid blue polo shirt—a step up from his normal summer's day-off attire of athletic shorts and T-shirt—he drove across town. He found a parking spot in the visitors' area and walked briskly through the courtyard to Tower Two. The air-conditioned lobby felt good after his brief walk in the Kansas summer heat. Crossing to the panel of intercom buttons, he located the one for the Cassidy apartment and buzzed. After only a few seconds, a crackly voice came through the speaker.

"This is Eileen."

He leaned forward and spoke into the microphone. "Eileen, this is Ben. I wondered if I could visit with Angela."

"Just a minute."

The *thwip* indicated the intercom flipped off. Minutes passed while he stood beside the row of buttons, alternately adjusting his collar and tugging the legs of his cargo shorts. *Maybe I should have run an iron over the twill. . . .*

"Ben?"

He'd expected a voice from the intercom, not from behind him. He spun around, banging his elbow on the wall.

"Whoops." A smile teased the corners of Angela's lips. "Sorry. I didn't mean to startle you."

"No problem." He rubbed his elbow and took a step toward her. She'd done something different with her hair—pulled it up in a rubber band where it spilled out like a fountain of shining curls on the top of her head. He liked it. "I didn't expect you to come down. I could've come up."

Her smile grew. "No, you couldn't. Aunt Eileen is mopping floors, and she didn't want you to see her in her mopping clothes."

"Oh, okay. And you aren't helping?"

Angela sighed. "She won't let me. She says guests aren't supposed to clean."

"Yeah, Eileen can be pretty stubborn."

"I'll say!"

His gaze flicked over her outfit. Although less dressy than what she wore to work each day, she still looked nice in the flowered skirt that fell just above the knee and bright yellow tank top. Not something one would wear to mop floors, he supposed.

"What did you need?" She brought him back to the task at hand.

He drew in a breath. "Let's go sit down, huh?"

A brief, puzzled scowl creased her forehead, but she turned toward the seating arrangement in the large lobby. Her jeweled flip-flops softly smacked her heels as she walked in front of him. She sat at one end of the sofa, and Ben chose the other end.

Facing her, he said, "I wanted to talk to you about Kent."

She settled in the corner and tucked her feet beside her. Her elbow on the back of the sofa, she rested her cheek against her fist. "What about him?"

"Well. . ." Ben scratched his head. "He said something kind of—worrisome—after you left yesterday evening. I wondered if you could shed any light on it."

Her shoulder lifted in a graceful shrug. "What did he say?"

"That you were his girlfriend."

She flashed a smile that lit her eyes. "Oh, that's really sweet."

Sweet? Ben frowned. "To be honest, Angela, it concerns me."

"Why should it?"

Could she really not understand the problem here? Surely she hadn't deliberately set out to mislead Kent. "Did you do something to give him the idea you would be his girlfriend?"

She sat upright, planting her fist against the sofa cushion between them. "What do you mean, did I 'do' something?"

The defensiveness took Ben by surprise. "There's no need to get angry. But you have to understand, while Kent's muscles and mind don't necessarily work like any typical male, his feelings are very much 'normal.'"

"I'm aware of that."

Her words snapped out on a harsh note Ben hadn't heard from her before. His own tone took a firmer quality. "Look, Angela, you can't—"

"I can't what? Talk to him? Be friends with him?"

Ben took a deep breath. This wasn't going very well. "You have to be careful. Kent's been hurt—a lot. Rejection is hard on him. If he thinks you're his girlfriend when you're really only—"

"Leading him on?" She leaned forward, her face inches from his, and nearly snarled. "That's what you think, isn't it?"

Ben hoped his face wasn't as red as it felt. "Well, I—"

Flopping back into the corner of the couch, she flipped her hands outward. "Great, just great. I work so hard at getting over my apprehensions about being around the handicapped, and the first time I feel truly comfortable with someone, I get accused of being a tease."

Ben listened, but he got the impression she was talking to herself more than him.

Before he could say anything, she swung around to face him again.

"If you want the truth, Ben, I do like Kent. I think he's a pretty nice guy. Great sense of humor, and I can tell he tries hard to do the best he can with what he's got to work with. I admire that. But as for being his girlfriend, no, I didn't tell him I'd be his girlfriend, and I didn't flirt with him. I'm sorry if he got that impression, and I'll try to kindly set him straight when I see him next."

She pointed a finger at his chest. "Because I will see him

again. I consider him a friend, and more than that, he reminds me that 'there but for the grace of God, go I.'"

Ben crunched his brows downward. "What do you mean by that?"

Her face flooded with pink, and she shot to her feet. "Never mind. You just remember what else I said. I'm going to be friends with Kent, and you can't stop me!"

Ben sat in openmouthed silence as she thundered to the elevators, her flip-flops smacking the tiled floor. She jabbed the elevator button, stood with crossed arms while staring at the silver doors, and then shot through the opening without a backward glance.

&

Angela stomped down the hallway that led to Aunt Eileen's apartment. Who did he think he was, accusing her of leading Kent on? Wasn't he the one who'd put in her evaluation that she needed to loosen up around the clients, to be more natural? Well, what had she done? She'd loosened up, treated Kent like she would any other male she encountered on the street, and now that was wrong, too!

Banging through the apartment door, she bellowed, "I'm back!" She gave the door a slam that probably echoed throughout the entire building.

Roscoe zipped out from under the end table and dashed down the hallway, yellow fur on end and tail puffed to twice its normal size.

Aunt Eileen appeared in the doorway between the kitchen and living room. The knot on the scarf she'd tied around her head stuck straight up like a bow. Beneath the scarf, her wrinkled face crunched in worry. "Angela, what's with the fireworks?"

Angela stormed from one end of the living room to the other, fists raised, emitting growls of frustration. Aunt Eileen captured her on the second pass and pushed her into the recliner. When she would have jumped to her feet, Aunt Eileen stood in front of her and crossed her arms, feet widespread.

"Uh-uh. Sit."

The firm look on her aunt's face held her in the chair. She slumped back, popped up the footrest, and crossed her ankles. "Fine. I'll sit."

Aunt Eileen gave her one more puzzled scowl before sitting on the arm of the couch. "All right. Spill it."

Angela huffed. "That. . .Ben!"

A smirk twisted Aunt Eileen's lips. "Oh."

Angela huffed louder. "No, not 'oh.' At least not like you said it." Kicking the footrest down, she sat up, put her elbows on her knees, and covered her face. "Why can't I ever do things right?"

"Wait a minute. Back up." Aunt Eileen grabbed one of Angela's hands and pulled it down. "What didn't you do right?"

A grunt of frustration found its way from Angela's chest. "Might be easier to make a list of what I have done right. It would take me all of—oh, three seconds—to name it off." She jabbed one finger in the air. "Coming here while Mom and Dad are away—that's about all I can think of that I've done right."

Although she'd promised to sit, she bounced to her feet again. "But done wrong? Oh, boy, can I list those! Hosted all those parties with the sole intention of rattling Dad's cage so he'd pay some attention to me. Ended up with guests who liked using stuff the policemen frown about." She thumped her own forehead with the butt of her hand. "Used the stuff myself. Duh! What is that—three things not done right?"

She began ticking off offenses on her fingers. "Then there's not only using but getting caught, getting sent to rehab, getting sent to community service at a place where I have to relate to people who are completely different than me—and doing it very badly."

"Hold up there." Aunt Eileen remained perched, her gaze pinned to Angela's face. "Why do you think you've done badly? Philip says you're working well there."

Angela stared at her aunt. "He said that?"

Aunt Eileen nodded, the knot on her head bobbing. "Yes, he did. He's pleased with your progress."

"Huh!" Angela thought about that for a moment, but then Ben's evaluation ran through her mind, bringing another scowl. "Well, according to Ben—who is my direct supervisor—I'm not doing things right." Once more, she began to pace.

Aunt Eileen reached out and grabbed her hand, bringing her to a halt. "Sweet girl, sit down. Please."

With a long sigh, Angela sank back into the recliner.

"Now." Aunt Eileen slid from the armrest to the couch seat. "Tell me exactly what happened downstairs with Ben. You weren't down there more than five minutes. He couldn't have possibly picked you apart in that short amount of time."

Oh, Angela only wished that statement weren't true. She felt tears gather in her eyes, and she blinked rapidly to control them. "Ben told me Kent said I was his girlfriend."

Aunt Eileen smiled, giving a wink and nod. "Ah, I can see why Kent would want that. You're a very pretty girl."

Angela brushed the comment aside. She didn't feel pretty right now. "He didn't seem happy about it. He asked me what

I was doing with Kent—like I'd been flirting with him." She pressed her palms to her chest. "I know I've been a flirt in the past, Aunt Eileen. I did a lot of things that weren't right before I became a Christian, but I'm trying so hard to change, to let people know Jesus is in my heart now."

"Of course you are." Aunt Eileen patted Angela's arm. "I've seen it."

She lowered her hands to her lap, twisting her fingers together. "I thought Ben knew it, that he saw it, but I guess not. I just want to be friends with Kent. I'd like to be friends with Ben, but I don't think he really trusts me. All he sees is this dumb woman who can't relax around people with handicaps. And I just don't see the point of trying if all I'm going to do is fail!"

Her voice fell silent, and Aunt Eileen remained quiet, too, her lips puckered in a thoughtful expression. Roscoe peeked from the hallway, his tail twitching, then made three running leaps to land beside Aunt Eileen's hip. He coiled into a ball and began to purr, his motor a soothing sound.

Angela sighed, her emotions spent. "Aunt Eileen, I'm so. . . alone. Mom and Dad are never around. My sisters. . . They've got their own lives. I'm staying away from my old friends so I don't get myself into trouble, but I really miss them. I miss the fun we used to have. Well, some of the fun. And what scares me is—when Ben accused me of coming on to Kent, I realized the old Angela is still hiding somewhere inside. What if she comes back? What if the need for friendship and fun takes me right back to where I was before?"

"That *won't* happen."

Angela laughed. Her aunt's adamant retort was encouraging, but she wasn't sure it was realistic. "How can you be sure?"

"Because you aren't the way you were before." Aunt Eileen leaned over the armrest of the sofa to clasp Angela's hand. "When you asked Jesus into your heart, He washed you clean. He made you holy. Now you just have to walk like you believe it."

"You mean, I should always be holy? I should never make mistakes?" Angela's heart gave a nervous double beat with that idea. If she were supposed to be free of mistakes, she had a long way to go.

"Now, I didn't say that. Unfortunately, we're humans, and humans aren't perfect." Aunt Eileen paused, her forehead creased in thought. "No, what I mean is you shouldn't spend your time worrying about what mistakes you might make. You should concentrate on two things. First, you aren't alone anymore. The Holy Spirit is with you, helping you be strong when you feel weak. When you're tempted, you just ask for help, and help will come. The Bible says we'll never be tested beyond our ability to resist. So remember that.

"And second, you've got me. I know I'm no young hipster, and it's not the same as having friends your age to hang up on—"

Angela burst out laughing. "Hang out with, Aunt Eileen!"

The older woman gave a tug on Angela's hand. "All right, all right, so I don't even know the terminology. But I'm here. I love you, and anytime you need something, you can come to me."

Angela thought her heart might melt. The tears returned. "Oh, Aunt Eileen, thank you. I love you, too."

"But just keep this in mind." Aunt Eileen's voice took on a stern undertone. "You don't have to depend on me. If there's a lesson I've learned well over the years, it's that there is One who will never abandon me, never turn a deaf ear, never refuse me comfort, and He's Jesus. Lean on Him, sweet girl, and you'll be fine."

Angela laid her head against the backrest of the old recliner and sighed. "How did you learn all this, Aunt Eileen? How do I get to be as—as comfortable with Jesus as you are?"

A smile lit her aunt's eyes. "Why, same way as with any relationship. Time. Think about your first days at New Beginnings. It was awkward, wasn't it?"

Angela nodded. She had been certain she wouldn't last ten minutes, let alone ten months.

"But what happened?" Aunt Eileen smiled, offering a wink. "You got to know the clients. You formed a relationship with them. And then the awkwardness slowly went away. That's the way it is with Jesus, too. You gotta talk to Him—get to know Him."

Angela nodded, nibbling her lower lip. Prayer. . . Carrie had said that, too. Reading the Bible every day and praying were important things for growing in the Christian walk.

She stood. "Aunt Eileen, I'm going to my room now. I–I'm going to do a little talking with Jesus."

eight

Angela rose from her knees at the side of the little bed in her temporary bedroom. Sitting on the edge of the mattress, she released a contented sigh. Aunt Eileen was right—talking to Jesus did make a person feel better. She raised her gaze to the ceiling and added a quick postscript: "I'll talk with You again soon. Count on it."

She rustled around in the half-unpacked suitcase at the end of the bed and located a pad of paper and pen. A list. . . While praying, she'd gotten the idea of forming a list of Christian friends who could be a support to her. She knew she shouldn't spend time with her old crowd. That could prove to be unwholesome. But somehow she needed to replace those relationships. Replacing them with Christian people seemed a wise thing to do.

Flipping the pad open, she wrote Christian Support System at the top of the page then began plugging in names. Aunt Eileen's name came first, followed by Carrie and her husband Rocky. Her boss, Philip, came next. And then her hand paused, the pen nib against the paper. Should she include Ben? He was a Christian, and he'd been a support up until that morning when he'd frustrated her so badly.

Her reaction to him replayed in her mind, and remorse struck. She shouldn't have barked at him like she had. Even if she were angry, she should have kept a rein on her tongue. She knew she hadn't spoken in a way pleasing to God.

Releasing a deep sigh, she contemplated digging her cell phone from her purse and calling him to apologize. Experiences from her past stung her memory. Some of what Ben intimated— her penchant for flirting—was accurate. She'd done so many foolish things. The inability to change them now brought a rush of frustration. Would she pay forever for the mistakes of her past? Although the desire to apologize was strong, the desire to protect herself from further condemnation won out. She didn't reach for her phone.

But she did add Ben's name to her list. At the bottom.

≈

Ben leaned back in his chair and bit down on the inside of his cheeks to keep from laughing. Angela and three clients sorted a stack of clean recyclables, and the confusion of the activity was enough to make a grown man cry. Yet there she was, with her shining head of hair all tousled, directing the chaos as well as a traffic cop directed the noon rush.

"Now, Pete, plastic goes in the middle bin. See? This says PLASTIC. Ketchup bottles are plastic. Yes, I know there's a picture of a tomato on the front just like the one on that can, but see? We have to look at what's under the picture. This is tin." She clinked her fingernail against the can. "And this is plastic." Thunking a finger against the bottle, she demonstrated the differences in the materials. "Do you understand? Now hold up, Jannie, we're not going to start a band here!"

Ben could barely contain his laughter as each of the clients chose an item or two from the bins to *clink* and *thud*. Angela's sweet laughter rang over the top of the noise. Finally she managed to convince everyone to put the "instruments" away and return to sorting. Her smile covered any hint of reprimand, and the clients each giggled, delivering friendly pats on Angela's back to show their willingness to cooperate.

Ben shook his head. How far she'd come. . . Based on his observations of her first couple of weeks, he would never have imagined her ever settling in. Yet she had, and he realized it was largely due to her commitment to emulate Jesus. He'd observed her attentiveness in church and Sunday school, and her focus during her Bible reading on her break was nearly impenetrable.

Although they hadn't spoken to one another except in passing since his visit to Elmwood Towers almost a week ago, he had continued to pray for her daily. Lifting her in prayer helped him feel connected to her even if she had pulled away.

The bell at the front door tinkled, announcing someone's entrance. Ben shifted his gaze to the door and spotted the center's owner, Philip Wilder, striding through. Philip paused beside the sorting table and visited with Angela for a moment. The beaming smile she aimed at him made Ben's heart lurch. He'd missed having that smile turned in his direction.

Philip laughed at something, gave Angela's arm a quick squeeze, and then walked to Ben's desk. Leaning against the desk's edge, he used his head to gesture toward the sorting table. "They're having fun over there, aren't they?"

Ben watched for another few seconds—long enough to see Pete try to put an empty butter tub on Angela's head for a hat and Angela return the favor—before answering Philip. "Oh, yeah, but I think in the midst of their fun, they're figuring out what needs to be done."

Philip nodded, chuckling, his gaze on the group. "Yes. I'm glad now I followed Carrie's recommendation. Angela's placement is working out better than I had anticipated."

Ben sent Philip a sharp look. "Placement? What do you mean by that?"

Philip gave a start. He jerked his gaze in Ben's direction, and he pulled his lips into a grimace. "It doesn't matter." He turned away, seeming to concentrate on the group at the recycling table.

Curiosity got the best of Ben. He stood and rounded the desk to stand next to Philip. "No, really. What did you mean by placement? Our clients go into different placements, not our workers. Are you starting something new?"

Philip blew out a breath. "Ben, really, it's not important."

"It is to me." Ben folded his arms across his chest and looked into Philip's face, even though the other man kept his gaze averted. "If we're starting some sort of new program, training people to work with the handicapped population, I'd like to know that. It will make a difference in how I evaluate their performances."

Finally Philip faced Ben. "You won't need to change how you evaluate performances. We aren't turning into a training center for anyone other than the people with disabilities. I said 'placement' for Angela because she technically isn't a hired employee."

Ben's eyebrows rose. "Isn't hired? You mean, she's unpaid—a volunteer?" His heart gave a lurch. If she were volunteering here, he'd been entirely too hard on her. He owed her a thank-you for her service, not criticism.

But Philip shook his head. "Not a volunteer. She's here as. . . community service."

Ben's jaw dropped. Community service? A judge would make that determination, which meant Angela had broken some kind of law. He glanced quickly at Angela. She handed a cereal box to Jannie then nodded in approval when the other woman dropped it in the appropriate bin. She'd broken the law? He felt his stomach clench.

"What did she do?"

"That, my friend, is confidential." Philip put his hand on Ben's shoulder. "Look, Ben, I wasn't even supposed to let you know her employment here is temporary and court-dictated. I'd appreciate it if you would keep it to yourself. It could alter her relationships with the other employees as well as the clients."

"But is it safe to have her here?" Ben hated himself for asking the question, yet he couldn't seem to stop himself.

Philip released a low chuckle. "If it weren't, she wouldn't be here." He pushed off from the desk. "Frankly, I think it's done Angela a world of good to be part of the staff at New Beginnings. It's given her a 'new beginning' of sorts, too. As I said earlier, it's worked out better than I'd hoped. I call it a God-thing."

Ben wasn't so sure about that, but he wouldn't argue with his boss. He nodded, but the thought tormented him the rest of the afternoon. Angela had broken the law and been given a sentence of community service. *What secret is she hiding?*

&

"Pizza again!" Ben announced as he entered Kent's apartment for their standard Friday night get-together.

Kent's eyes lit up. He sniffed the air like a bloodhound. "Pep–peron–i and pep–pers?"

Ben laughed. "You know your pizza. Yep. Added peppers this time." He carried the box to the living room and dropped it on the low table beside the couch. "Want to eat in front of the TV?"

Kent nodded and pushed the chair to the end of the table. With a low grunt, he managed to lean forward far enough to get hold of the remote control. Aiming the black box at the television, he pushed buttons until he located a baseball game. He crowed with excitement. "Home run!"

Ben headed to the kitchen to retrieve paper towels and get a grip on his emotions. Sorrow pressed his chest at Kent's elation at watching the sport he'd once loved to play. Kent had been the champion home-run hitter on their junior high baseball team. His mother had taken down the trophy from the shelf in the family room, but Ben knew it was hidden somewhere in the house. He should ask for it, bring it over, and put it on top of the television. Kent might enjoy having it.

He handed a wad of paper towels to his cousin then sank down on the sofa. Although Kent was already munching, he lowered his head and offered a brief prayer of thanks before picking up a piece of pizza. He got as caught up in the game as Kent, cheering for the pitcher and booing when the ump made a poor call. At one point, the camera zoomed in on the scoreboard where, for a few seconds, the score disappeared and was replaced with the image of a pair of spectators—two women wearing baseball caps and waving banners.

Ben whistled and poked Kent with his elbow. "Hey, some pretty girls, huh? What do you think, Kent?"

Kent shook his head, scowling. "An—ge—la is. . .pretty." He grinned. "She. . .is my. . . girlfriend. She visits. . .me."

Ben fought the wave of worry that welled up. Keeping an intentionally light tone, he said, "Oh, yeah? When does she visit you?"

"Work. Home from. . .work." Kent chomped down on another bite of pizza. "I see her. . .in lobby."

The worry from earlier in the day magnified with this new information. Apparently she hadn't heeded his warning about Kent's misinterpretation of her intentions. Remembering how she'd spouted her intent to be friends with Kent, he felt his ire grow. *Stubborn woman! Can't she listen to reason?* And now that he knew she'd been found guilty of a crime that warranted community service as a punishment, he was even more concerned about Kent spending time with her.

Since Angela hadn't made Kent understand a relationship beyond friendship wasn't possible, he was left with the difficult task of crushing his cousin. He took a deep breath, prayed for the right words, and tapped Kent's arm.

"Hey, Kent?"

Kent pulled his gaze away from the television and offered a little grunt at the interruption of the game.

"I have to tell you something. . .about Angela."

"An–ge–la?" The expectant look in his cousin's eyes took Ben back fifteen years to seventh grade and the first all-school party. Kent had had a crush on Macie Warren, and he'd sent Ben over to see if she'd go with him to the party. Macie said no, and Ben had been faced with telling Kent the bad news. He could still see the eager hope in Kent's eyes as he'd walked back from the giggling group of girls.

He swallowed. It was just as hard today as it had been back then. "You see, Kent, Angela is a real nice girl, but. . ." He took in another fortifying breath. "She really isn't your girlfriend, is she?"

Kent began rocking in his wheelchair, his face tightening into a scowl.

Ben grabbed his arm to make him sit still.

Kent jerked loose, his scowl deepening. "An–ge–la is. . .my. . . girlfriend," he spat the words.

Ben shook his head. "Your friend, Kent. Your friend, but not your girlfriend."

Swinging his hand, Kent whacked the pizza box from the table. The remaining two pieces flew to the floor, one upside down. "You go!"

The anger tore at Ben's heart. "Listen, Kent, I'm not trying to upset you, but—"

"Go! Go! Go!" Kent repeated the word at top volume, his face red, until his voice sounded hoarse.

Someone knocked on the door, and it swung open before Ben could get up. Kent's resident caretaker rushed into the room. She seemed surprised to see Ben sitting on the couch. "What's going on?"

"Go!" Kent yelled again, pointing a finger at Ben.

The caretaker crouched beside Kent's wheelchair. "Kent, I'll take Ben outside. You calm down, okay? When he's outside, will you be all right?"

Kent nodded his head, his hair flopping. "Ben. . .go!"

The woman stood and grabbed Ben's arm to escort him to the hallway. After closing the door, she said, "What happened in there? I haven't seen Kent that upset in ages!"

Ben hung his head. "I told him something he didn't want to hear." His heart ached. His cousin's fury spoke so clearly of the pain Ben had caused.

"Was it necessary to tell him?"

Ben nodded. "Yeah. I really believe it was."

"Well, from past experience, I know it won't take him long to calm down if we give him some space." She sighed, looking toward the closed door. "I'll stay here and listen. If it sounds as if he's tearing the place apart, I'll go right in. Otherwise, I'll give him ten minutes or so then help clean up the mess he made."

"Okay. Thanks for your help." Ben shoved his hands into his pants pockets.

"Do you mind telling me what you said to get him so upset? I might be able to smooth the waters for you."

"This woman who's staying in Tower Two has given him the idea that she's his girlfriend, and—"

"You mean Angela?"

Ben frowned. "You know her?" Just how often had Angela come around?

The caretaker nodded. "Yes. She's great with Kent. She gets him talking, and they've taken long walks all over the grounds in the evenings. I've never seen her be anything but appropriate with him though."

Ben stood for a moment, uncertain whether or not to believe her. Maybe he'd misjudged Angela. But there was still the issue of community service. Even if she hadn't been deliberately misleading with Kent, he had big concerns about the reason for her sentence.

"That may be," he finally said, choosing his words carefully, "but somehow Kent's gotten the idea there's more than friendship between them. It needs to be nipped now before he really gets hurt."

"You might be right on that." The caretaker sighed. "As much as I hate to get in the middle of friendships, part of my job is to protect Kent. I'll see if I can keep some distance between the two of them. At least until we can get Kent's feelings sorted out."

Ben heaved a sigh of relief. "Thank you."

The caretaker patted his arm. "Go on home, Ben. It sounds like Kent has settled down. I'll go in and sit with him for a while."

"Okay. Thanks again." Ben waited until the caretaker went into Kent's apartment before heading to the elevators. Riding down alone, his thoughts turned once more to Angela. The caretaker's description of her time with Kent made him regret his subtle accusation, yet at the same time he still felt uncertain whether or not to trust her with his cousin.

The elevator doors opened to the lobby, and he headed to the doors leading outside, his mind running for ways to prove or disprove Angela's suitability to be with Kent. He'd tried twice to talk to Angela about her life before starting work at New Beginnings. Both times she'd sidestepped his questions and turned the conversation elsewhere. There were many unanswered questions hovering in Ben's mind.

For the sake of Kent's protection, he had to know what Angela had done to warrant a sentence of community service. He needed one-on-one time with her if he intended to un-cover her secrets. He slipped behind the wheel of his truck, a decision made. Tomorrow after church, he'd invite her to lunch. Just the two of them.

By the time Sunday afternoon arrived, he'd have his answers. No matter what it took.

nine

Ben trotted across the parking area to catch Angela before she climbed behind the wheel of the silver rocket. Amazing how fast she could move through the muggy August heat on those high-heeled strappy shoes.

"Whew, I caught you!" He came to a halt beside the driver's door and grabbed the frame before she could pull it closed.

"Did you need something?"

The apprehension in her gaze troubled him, but he pushed the feeling aside. "Yeah. I wondered if you had lunch plans."

She shrugged. "Not really. Why?"

"Want to go somewhere?" He shrugged, too, feeling as tongue-tied as a nervous teenager. "Grab a bite with me?"

She looked at him for a long time, her expression puzzled, while he squirmed under the silent perusal. Finally she sighed. "I should probably call Aunt Eileen and make sure it's okay."

He waved a hand. "That's fine. I'll wait." He turned his back and pretended not to listen to the one-sided conversation.

"Aunt Eileen? Hi, I just wondered if it would be okay if I didn't come back to the apartment for lunch. . . . I'm not sure. Ben asked if I'd like to get something with him. No, it probably won't be too late." She laughed softly, causing fresh sweat to break out under his arms. Why did he wish she'd use that soft tone with him? "Sure, I can be quiet when I come in. I know you and Roscoe like your Sunday afternoon nap. Okay, see you soon. Bye."

He turned around in time to see her snap the phone closed, smiling to herself. When she looked up and met his gaze, her smile faded. "Where did you want to go?"

The need to bring the smile back hit him hard. He reminded himself of the purpose of this lunch. "I like that little submarine shop on Fourth and Main. Have you been there?" He knew it wasn't fancy, but the high backs on the booths provided a small measure of privacy. And they had a mean cherry cheesecake—perfect comfort food.

She shrugged again, the curls that fell across her shoulders bouncing with the movement. "That's fine. I'll meet you there." Without another word, she closed her door and started the engine.

He stepped back to allow her passage then jogged to his truck. He chuckled to himself as he turned the key in the ignition. If she drove as quickly as she walked, she'd be there long before he was. Fortunately, he was able to pass a vehicle and fall in behind her. They pulled between slanting white lines and got out at the same time.

He double-stepped past her to open the door to the sub shop. The sweet rush of air-conditioning carried a yeasty smell that made Ben's stomach writhe in desire. He noticed Angela draw in a deep breath, too.

They placed their orders at the serving counter, and then he carried their tray of sandwiches, chips, and drinks to a booth tucked in the corner. The sun glared on the large plate-glass window, but the vent overhead whirred, promising to keep them cool.

Ben waited until Angela slid in on one side, tucking her skirt underneath her in a feminine manner. He put the tray down and sat across from her, careful to keep his big feet well back. Once he was settled, he said, "Would you like me to pray?"

She nodded in reply, and he closed his eyes and offered a short blessing. He handed her the paper-wrapped sandwich marked "turkey/provolone" and took the one with "roast beef/cheddar" written on the wrapper. They each opened a small bag of chips and began munching.

After allowing her time to take a few bites, Ben rested his elbows on the edge of the table and said, "So have you lived in Petersburg your whole life?"

Angela blotted her lips with her napkin. "Yes, I was born here." She took another bite.

"Is it a good place to grow up?"

She swallowed, blotted again, and answered, "I suppose. I don't have anything to compare it with. Where did you grow up?"

"A half hour south of here, in Liberal."

"What brought you to Petersburg?"

Ben realized he was getting sidetracked. Again. His intention was to find out about Angela, not for Angela to find out about him. But he couldn't be rude and not answer. He gave her the shortened version. "A job and Elmwood Towers."

At her confused look, he laughed and expanded the information. "I heard about the assisted-living apartments at Elmwood Towers and applied for Kent to move into one. When I helped him move in, I met your aunt Eileen, who told me Philip Wilder was looking for a new manager since she'd given up the position to be a resident caretaker at the Towers." He shrugged. "It was just the kind of job I wanted, and my degree in social services qualified me. God worked it all out."

She nodded slowly.

"Do you have a college degree?"

Her face pinched as though the question pained her, and she set her sandwich down, smoothing the paper wrapper flat against the table. "Yes, I do. But it isn't in social services." She didn't offer further explanation.

Ben headed in another direction, one he was certain would open up the door to understanding. "I haven't seen your friend for a while."

She tipped her head. "Friend?"

"Yeah. The man who visited you a couple of weeks ago. . . I didn't catch his name."

Immediately she lowered her gaze, tucking her lower lip between her teeth. He knew he'd hit upon a tender spot.

"Is your relationship with him. . .significant?" His heart pounded while he waited for a response. But he assured himself the thudding evidenced the depth of his curiosity, nothing more.

Without looking up, she said, "Significant but short-term."

The cryptic reply only increased his interest in the subject. He forced a light chuckle. "You know that already, huh?"

She flashed a quick look at him. "Yes. I know that." Sighing, she pushed her food away and raised her chin to meet his gaze directly. "Ben, what's your motive for inviting me here?"

He felt heat climb his neck. If he answered honestly, she'd no doubt run out the door. But he couldn't lie to her and say he had no reason. Words wouldn't form on his tongue. He sat in tense silence, feeling trapped beneath her gaze.

After several long seconds, she released another, regret-filled sigh. "I know what you're trying to get me to tell you. And to be perfectly honest, I'm tired of sneaking around. You want the truth, Ben? Here it is. . ."

Angela saw Ben's shoulders stiffen, and it furthered her belief that he'd simply been sitting there, information tucked neatly away, waiting for her to confirm what he already knew. *Okay, Lord, here I go. . . .*

She continued, deliberately keeping her gaze fixed on Ben's penetrating blue eyes. "That man who came to see me isn't a boyfriend. He isn't even a friend. He's my court-appointed probation officer. He came that day to administer a random drug test. I will have at least three more of them before my sentence is up. I have to submit to them because I was convicted of illegal drug use."

Ben's eyebrows shot so high they almost became part of his short-cropped hairline. He did a good job of looking surprised; she'd give him that.

"I was given a one-year sentence, part of which was a requirement to go to a rehabilitation center. I've been through drug rehab, but I have to serve ten months of community service. I'm doing that at New Beginnings." Her mouth felt dry. She lifted her soda cup and took a drink. Ben remained silent, his face unreadable, as she continued.

"You want more truth? My life was hardly lily-white before I got caught. I've done a lot of stupid things, starting in high school. Drinking, skipping school, and—as you've already figured out—enjoying the company of men."

Ben's neck blotched red, and she felt her own face flood with fire as she recognized his interpretation of her confession. She leaned forward. "I never did anything. I wasn't that stupid! But I teased a lot. Enjoyed it, too—the power of it." She released a rueful laugh. "Between my mama's good looks and my daddy's money, there weren't too many boys who weren't interested in spending time with me."

The shame of her past hit again, shrinking her into the seat. She lowered her gaze. "I got my college degree in art history just because I knew it was something that would irritate my dad. He thought it was a waste of time and money. And he was right, because I have no desire to do anything with it. But at least when he was ranting at me, he wasn't ignoring me."

She shrugged, shifting her gaze to peer out the window at the sunshiny day. Watching two sparrows battle over a crumb on the sidewalk, she finished. "And that's why I started using the drugs. I thought maybe Dad would—I don't know—rescue me. That's all I really wanted—a dad to rescue me."

Ben didn't say anything in response. After a few moments of silence, she looked at him. The censure in his eyes stung like a lash. She dropped her gaze to the tabletop so she wouldn't have to see his expression. But it burned in her memory.

Eyes downcast, she finished in a hoarse whisper. "So there you have it, Ben. All my ugly secrets." Suddenly a wave of courage washed over her. Although she had no desire to be subjected to his disdain, she needed him to see her face when she spoke the final truth. She lifted her face and met his steely gaze.

"But you know what? The drug use finally got me what I wanted—Someone to rescue me. Only it wasn't my dad who did it, it was my Father. God rescued me, Ben. I met His Son, and I invited Him into my heart. I've got Him now, and even though I made a total mess of things, He loves me anyway. And I won't ever let Him down by doing something so stupid as abusing my body again."

Ben still didn't say anything. There was something indefinable lurking behind his blue-eyed gaze. Disappointment, certainly, but something else. Something deeper. Suddenly Angela didn't want to pursue it.

"Thank you for the sandwich, but I've got to go." Her dignity in shreds, she slipped from the booth and ran out of the restaurant. As she pulled away from the curb, she saw Ben, still in the booth, staring outward. She blinked to clear the tears from her vision and forced her gaze forward.

Back at the apartment, she nearly ran through the foyer, her heels clicking a rapid tempo against the tile floor. Two residents called hello from the seating area. She raised a hand in a quick wave and charged into the elevator without pausing to chat. She held her breath, her chest so tight she thought she might explode. Not until she'd sealed herself in Aunt Eileen's apartment did she finally release the air she'd been holding.

And tears followed. Rivers of tears accompanied by huge, gulping sobs that doubled her over. She collapsed on the sofa, curled into a ball, and let the torrent run its course. Not since her first night in drug rehab had she cried this hard. She wasn't even sure why she was crying; she just knew the emotions couldn't be held back.

When the tears were spent, she stumbled to the bathroom and used several tissues to clean her face and blow her nose. Her head ached, and she fumbled around in the medicine cabinet until she located a bottle of aspirin. When she'd swallowed two of them with some water, she wandered back into the hallway.

Aunt Eileen's door was cracked open, and through the slit she spotted her aunt's bare feet sticking out from under a light blanket. Roscoe, at the end of the bed, raised his head and peered at her with round, yellow eyes. He offered a short *meow*, yawned, and lay back down.

Carefully she pulled the door all the way closed, relieved she hadn't wakened her aunt. Back in the living room, she curled in the recliner. Ben's face—with shocked disapproval in his eyes—appeared once more in her memory. Not even when she'd told him the good that had come of her drug abuse conviction, not even when she'd promised to never use drugs again, had his expression cleared.

Her head throbbed, and she massaged her temples. Closing her eyes, she whispered aloud, "Oh, Jesus, please replace Ben's face with Yours in my head. Remind me that You've forgiven me. Remind me that You love me unconditionally."

Another spurt of tears accompanied the simple prayer. But they weren't tears of anguish. They were tears of gratitude. Because Jesus answered.

ten

Ben remained in the booth, too stunned to get up. Only dimly aware of the chatter of other patrons, the hum of the air-conditioning, and the slow-moving traffic on the street outside the window, he sat replaying Angela's words.

She'd used drugs.

She'd been through drug abuse rehabilitation.

She'd said she wouldn't abuse her body that way again.

He shook his head. Oh, yes, she would. How many times had Kent gone through rehab? At least three. And every time he returned to the crutch of drug use. He was drug free now, but not from choice. He simply no longer had access to people who could provide drugs to him.

Except for Angela.

A part of Ben wanted to kick himself for even thinking Angela might provide drugs to Kent, yet the greater part of him—the part that had learned to protect his cousin—overrode the other. If Angela had used drugs in the past, she knew how to get them. If she knew how to get them, she knew how to share them.

He pinched the bridge of his nose between his thumb and fingers, trying to ignore the memory of her pleading eyes as she'd told him of her acceptance of Christ into her heart. Evidence of growth had been seen in the past weeks, especially since she'd begun attending church regularly. She certainly had the pull of God on her heart. But. . .

Ben hung his head, his chest tightening with the knowledge of how hard the tug of drugs could be. Hadn't he seen it with Kent? Kent had struggled against it, had vowed to give it up, had remained drug free for weeks, even months, at a time. . . but always, always, he'd gone back to the old habit.

It wasn't as if Ben believed drugs were stronger than God. He knew better. But he wasn't sure Angela was strong enough in her new faith to resist the habit. With wooden movements, he piled the half-eaten sandwiches and crumpled chips wrappers on the tray and carried it to the trash can.

When he got in his truck, he realized he didn't want to go home. The empty apartment held no appeal. He considered driving to Elmwood Towers and seeing if Kent wanted to go for a ride, but the fear of running into Angela made him nix that idea. Starting his engine, he pulled into the street and drove aimlessly. By force of habit, he turned on familiar streets and ended up at New Beginnings.

To his surprise, Philip's motorcycle sat in the parking area behind the warehouselike building. Curious, he pulled in next to the cycle and entered the building through the back door.

Philip looked up from his desk when Ben slammed the door. His face creased into a puzzled frown. "Hey, what are you doing here on a Sunday afternoon?"

"I was about to ask you the same thing." Ben dropped into the plastic chair facing his boss's desk. "Since when do you work on Sundays?"

Philip released a low chuckle and leaned back in his chair. He linked his fingers behind his head and rocked slightly, yawning. "I don't. But my lovely wife had a brainstorm about a fund-raising carnival for the winter Special Olympics, and I needed to check my schedule to see where it could be penciled in."

Ben glanced at the desk calendar in the middle of Philip's messy desk. Every square inch held scribbled reminders. "I assume you discovered you aren't available?"

Another chuckle. "I discovered I'm a busy man—as if I didn't already know it." He rocked in his chair, its squeaky springs loud in the quiet room. "So what are you doing here? I'm pretty sure Marin didn't give you any ideas to pursue."

Ben offered a small grin. "No, although I'll help in whatever way I can. I'm hoping Kent will participate in the winter Olympics basketball game, and maybe some of the wheelchair races in next summer's Special Olympics."

"That'd be great," Philip said. He brought his arms down and draped his elbows on the chair arms. "Angela mentioned he's been visiting the weight room at the Towers, and he's gone walking with her in the evenings after it has cooled down a bit. Sounds as if he's getting out a lot more."

The reminder of Angela spending time with Kent brought a new stab of worry. "Hey, Philip, I'm glad I caught you here. I need to talk to you about Angela." He paused, his gaze swinging through the empty building. It seemed sad and almost lonely with the normally busy stations devoid of clients and absent of Angela's bright hair and beaming smile. Turning back to Philip, he said, "She told me today why she's in community service."

Philip nodded, one eyebrow quirked. "I'm not surprised. I wondered how long she'd be able to keep it from you." He leaned forward, resting his forearms on the desk, and fiddled with a pen. "I've gotten the impression pleasing you has become pretty important to Angela—and not just because you're her supervisor."

Ben pulled his lips into a scowl. "If she'd like to please me, she should stay away from Kent."

Philip's hand stilled on the pen. "Has she mistreated Kent in some way?"

"As far as I know, she hasn't," Ben answered truthfully. "But that doesn't mean she won't."

Philip shook his head hard, a teasing grin twitching. He began rolling the pen beneath his palms. "You're going to have to elaborate on that comment. You just lost me."

Ben puffed his cheeks and blew. "She's an addict, Philip. She uses drugs."

"She *was* a drug user. Past tense." Philip's calm rejoinder did little to reassure Ben.

"I'm not so sure past tense exists when it comes to the addiction of drug use." Ben's heart clenched with his statement. He wished so much it weren't true.

"So you're saying Angela's profession of faith is fake?"

Ben looked sharply at Philip. "Her profession of faith has nothing to do with it."

"Ben!" A brief huff of laughter burst out. "It has everything to do with it."

Unable to find the words to express his thoughts, Ben sat silently.

Philip rolled the pen into a drawer, shut the drawer with a snap, and then linked his fingers together on the desktop. "Look, I think I understand where this concern is based. It's because of Kent, right? The fact that he kept returning to drugs?"

Ben shifted his gaze to the right, away from Philip's earnest face, and nodded.

"So your skepticism is logical. However, you're forgetting that logic doesn't always exist in the world of Jesus."

Ben's gaze jerked back to Philip. "Logic doesn't exist in the world of Jesus? Now *you* elaborate."

Philip shrugged. "How logical is it that a man who grew up bullying and tormenting others would open a business that serves the needs of the very people he used to bully? Yet I became a Christian, and God turned me around."

Ben felt his jaw drop. Philip? Kind Philip, a bully? The picture wouldn't gel. But bullying wasn't an addiction. He shook his head. "It's not the same thing."

"Yes, it is. 'The old has gone, the new has come!' Do you think there are limits on God? Only this thing can fade away, but that thing can't?"

Ben couldn't say he doubted the power of God. Yet, in his experience, a person's powerful desire for drugs could keep that person from leaning on God to resist the need. "I think God has the power to do anything, but I also think some people won't let Him."

Philip sat for a while, staring at Ben through narrowed eyes. Finally he nodded. "Okay. Yeah, I'll concede on that one. People sure can follow a wrong pathway. But"—he leaned forward, his gaze intent—"just because one chooses the wrong pathway doesn't mean they all will."

Ben shifted his gaze away again. Philip's quiet words hit like an arrow in a bull's-eye.

"Give Angela a chance. I've seen so much growth just in the few weeks she's been here. I know you've seen it, too. Can't you trust her when she says she's changed?"

"No." The word came from a throat that felt strangled.

Philip shrugged. "Okay. . ."

The chair squeaked again, and suddenly Philip stepped into Ben's line of vision. Ben met his employer's gaze. Philip's eyes contained no hint of condemnation for Ben's hard stance. Only compassion lingered there.

"Ben, there is a way to ease your fears."

"Fire Angela?" Ben forced a humorless chuckle.

Philip shook his head. "You know we can't do that. She wasn't hired. No hire, no fire." He gave a grin that Ben did his best to imitate. "But we can pray." He pulled a second plastic chair over and sat down, his knees a few inches from Ben's. Folding his hands in his lap, he said, "Marin and I were reading in Ephesians a few nights ago. The topic of holiness is expressed pretty beautifully in that book."

Ben's chin shot up. Ephesians. . .and holiness. . . His minister had spoken on holiness the first Sunday he'd taken Angela to church.

"I'm going to pray for Angela, for her to stand firm in her new convictions. But I'm also going to pray for you—for you to be able to see her as the holy creature God desires her to be." Without another word, he lowered his head and began to pray.

Ben closed his eyes and hunched forward, but the tightness in his chest held back the worries he longed to leave in his Father's hands.

&

Angela consulted the clipboard that held the day's schedule, using her finger to scan the list to locate her name. In the task column across from her name she read "mopping/table cleaning with Randy, Doris, and Anton." She sighed. Her least favorite tasks, and two of those delegated to her area were brand-new clients, which meant she would have a stressful day. Any change in routine was difficult for many of the New Beginnings clients.

Turning from the assignment board, she headed to her locker, her gaze bouncing past Ben. He kept his head down, just as he'd done the previous two days this week. His rejection hurt more than she wanted to admit.

She couldn't blame him for his disapproval. She certainly deserved it after the poor choices she'd made. Yet Ben's disapproval was harder to bear than any other—even more than her parents'. Their anger and disappointment was largely due to the fact that she had been foolish enough to get caught, thereby causing them embarrassment. Ben's disappointment was directly related to her behavior.

Placing her purse in the locker, she rested her hand on the Bible waiting on the shelf. Through prayer, she'd been able to find comfort for her aching heart each night as she stretched out on the bed in Aunt Eileen's spare room. But during the day, even though she was busy, the ache returned.

Loneliness hit hard. The last two evenings the caretaker for Kent's floor had turned her away when she'd come to visit Kent. Aunt Eileen was tied up in something with other ladies at her church and had been out. She'd consulted her list of "supporters" and refrained from bothering Carrie. What newlywed wants to spend evenings away from her husband? And she didn't know anyone from the Sunday school class at church well enough to call out of the blue to do something.

So she had been alone. Giving the locker a firmer slam than was necessary, she headed to the cleaning area. The tinkle of the bell announced the arrival of clients, and she greeted those with whom she would be working. Of the three, Anton seemed the most nervous. He hung back, peeking over Randy's shoulder, his round eyes wide behind his thick glasses.

Angela's heart went out to him. She smiled and offered a kind welcome, but he shrank away, making a noise of distress. Angela turned to Doris, the one familiar face among the three.

"Doris, would you like to show Randy and Anton where to find the mop buckets? We'll be scrubbing the floors today."

Doris nodded and looked at the two waiting men. "C'mon, you guys." She waved her chubby hand then scuttled toward the supply closet. With one more apprehensive look thrown at Angela, Anton followed. Randy trailed more slowly, his gait swaying. Angela walked beside him.

She worked with the trio all morning, showing them how to fill the bucket to the waterline and measure the cleaning agent, how to wring the excess water from the mop, and how to push the mop head across the floor. When Anton stepped on the long strings, she reached to assist him. But he pulled away, squeaking in fear.

By the time the lunch break arrived, her temples pounded, and she toyed with the idea of asking if she could leave early. Only knowing to gain permission she'd have to talk to Ben kept her from following through.

Despite her best efforts at patience and gentle teasing—things she'd discovered worked well with most clients—she made no progress at all in helping Anton feel comfortable. She nearly wilted with relief when the bus driver arrived to transport him home. She walked her charges to the door and said good-bye to each one, but only Doris offered any response.

At her locker, preparing to go home, her cell phone inside her purse blared out its song. She yanked it out and flipped up the lid. It took a minute before she recognized the number on the screen, but then a rush of eagerness filled her. She pushed the TALK button and squealed into the phone.

"Janine!"

"Hey, girl, long time no see."

Janine's voice, familiar and welcoming, made tears prick behind Angela's eyes. She pulled out a chair at the break table and sat down, cradling the phone against her cheek. "I know. How are you?"

"Ornery—same as always." Janine's laughter rang briefly.

Angela laughed, too. The first genuine laugh in days. It felt good. "Yeah? Well, I suppose the same applies to me."

"What did you do today?"

Angela replayed the monotonous tasks, the unresponsive clients. With a sigh, she said, "I mopped floors and washed tables."

To Janine's credit, she didn't make a smart remark, but Angela could hear humor in her tone as she said, "Sounds like. . .fun." There was a slight pause before she went on. "So, do you have time for your ol' buds?"

Angela licked her lips. She glanced up and, through the break in the partitions, she noticed Ben at his desk, his head bent over his work. Her heart caught. "Yeah. I've got time for you guys. What's up?"

"Todd, Alex, and me are meeting for pizza. Why don't you come? Fill us in on your adventures in Rehab Land." The laughter came again, and Angela ignored the brittle undertone.

"At the Ironstone?" Angela noticed Ben lift his head, and for one brief second their gazes met. She turned away before he did.

"Yep. At six. Can you make it?"

"Yeah, I can do that. I need to run by my aunt's apartment and change out of my work clothes though." She had finally resorted to jeans, T-shirts, and sneakers for work, but she couldn't show up at the Ironstone dressed so sloppily.

Janine's snort blasted Angela's ear. "I bet! We'll be there. See you soon." Angela clicked the phone closed and dropped it in her purse. Then she charged out the door.

eleven

Ben stared at the closed door, his heart thumping. Although the air-conditioning kept the building comfortably cool, he felt sweat break out on his body.

Who was Angela meeting? She was obviously comfortable with the person. He'd gathered that from the tone she'd used. What he hadn't been able to determine from the lopsided conversation was the purpose of the get-together. Was it possible she was meeting with her drug-using friends?

Ben ran his hand down his face, wondering what he should do. He was Angela's supervisor, not her keeper. Yet he was also her—

Swallowing, he processed where his thoughts were going. Should he consider her a friend? Or something more? He admitted that over the weeks she had worked at New Beginnings, he'd come to care about her. His time in prayer for her, attending Sunday school and church together, and their times of conversation had developed an undefined relationship.

As her supervisor, he had no authorization to check up on her outside of working hours. His authority was nonexistent there. However, as a Christian mentor, his concern was not only appropriate but warranted. Didn't the Bible say admonishment in love was a sign of Christian care and concern? Plus, if he took it a step further and considered her a friend, he had a real obligation to protect her. Possibly from herself.

But was there a reason to be worried?

Concern and curiosity wavered at the back of his mind as he went through the closing-down routine, checking the different training areas and locking closets. By the time he'd finished everything, the clock by the back door showed 6:05. Angela had intended to meet her mysterious friend at six. Ben paused, his hand on the doorknob, his gaze on the clock. The *tick-tick-tick* seemed loud in the otherwise quiet warehouse. The clock seemed to deliver a message: *Check-check-check. . .*

He released a disgruntled huff. He wouldn't be able to rest this evening unless he found out what Angela was doing with that friend at the Ironstone. It would only take a few minutes to run by the pizza place. But it might save him an evening of worry.

He climbed behind the wheel of his truck and headed for the Ironstone. Pulling behind the building, he spotted Angela's silver rocket in the far corner of the parking lot. It sent up a question—was she trying to conceal her presence? He trotted across the asphalt and entered the pizza restaurant.

Lights were dimmed, fat candles sending out minimal light in the center of each table. The room was crowded at the supper hour, most tables filled. He stepped further into the dining area and squinted, his gaze slowly sweeping the room. He knew he'd locate her by her clearly identifiable head of hair. Sure enough, he found her seated at a corner table, her back to the door. As he watched, she leaned sideways to say something to the man on her left, and Ben got a glimpse of a half-empty pitcher of amber liquid. Beer.

His stomach clenched. Alcohol consumption had been Kent's precursor to drug use. Her words from Sunday played through his head, "I won't ever let Him down by doing something so stupid as abusing my body again." Didn't her word mean anything? It was like Kent all over again.

The thought turned his stomach. He took two steps toward the table, his hands curling into fists. She shouldn't be here. He should haul her away. Remove her from the beer and the people and the situation. But then he stopped, taking in a deep breath to calm himself.

How much good had it done to haul Kent out of those kinds of situations? None. Hadn't he learned the hard way that one person couldn't control another person's behavior? Angela would have to decide for herself the choices she was making were wrong. His hauling her away would only lead to resentment, just as it had with Kent. It had nearly ruined his relationship with his cousin.

I can't go through this again, Lord. Suddenly he had no desire to stand here and witness her descent into drug use. His chest aching, he turned toward the door.

≈

"Come on, Angela, you haven't even had a sip." Todd lifted the pitcher and splashed beer into the empty mug waiting at the edge of Angela's paper place mat.

Angela pushed the mug toward the center of the table. "I don't want any, Todd."

Todd snorted.

Janine chided, "Don't be such a stick in the mud. It's lite, just like you always wanted. Drink up."

"Yeah," Alex agreed, smirking. "What happened to our Party Queen? You've become a real dud hanging out at New Beginnings."

The others shared a laugh, adding their own rude comments about New Beginnings' clientele. Images of the clients—

cheerful Steve, sweet Doris, bashful Randy—crowded Angela's mind. Protectiveness welled up, and she opened her mouth, ready to spew.

"Quit being a party pooper, Angela. Join us, huh? We've missed you." Janine's comment erased the planned speech from Angela's brain.

Angela stared at the clear, amber liquid. Drops of condensation formed on the glass mug, shimmering like diamonds in the flickering light of the candle. Her throat convulsed. Memories of past times—being in the middle of the action, accepted by the crowd—washed over her. Her fingers twitched as she contemplated reaching for the glass mug.

Planting both palms against the table edge, she pushed her chair backward. "I gotta make a little visit to the ladies' room. Be right back."

She fled the table, her heart pounding so hard she could feel it. As she rounded the corner leading to the restrooms, a movement by the front doors caught her attention. Her gaze jerked in that direction, and she recognized Ben's close-cropped hair and broad back as he headed out the door.

She slapped her hands to her face. Had he seen her at the table with the others? If so, what must he think? Making a rapid turn, she charged after him. She burst through the door, calling, "Ben!"

He looked over his shoulder, and his steps ceased. Turning around, he fixed her with an unsmiling stare. "Angela."

From the look on his face, she knew he'd seen everything. She pointed to the restaurant. "It isn't what you're thinking."

He folded his arms, his brows coming down in a disapproving scowl.

Placing her hands against her chest to force down the wave

of guilt, she assured him, "I was just sitting with them. I didn't drink anything."

He still didn't answer. Yet his expression said as much as a lecture.

Anger at his condescending attitude filled her, dispelling any guilt. What right did he have to sit in judgment on her? He had friends, people with whom he could spend time. What did he know of loneliness?

Plunking her fists on her hips, she glared upward. "Look, Ben, I have a right to see my friends. Do you have any idea how much my life has changed? I used to be the center of everything, always involved in small group get-togethers and big parties. People called me to go grab a drink or go shopping or take a drive. Now? Nothing! Not since rehab."

Pointing toward the restaurant again, she continued in a harsh tone. "So I decided to meet some old friends for supper. So they decided to drink beer with their pizza. What difference should that make? It's not like I'm sitting there getting drunk with them."

Ben's stern countenance softened. He dropped his cross-armed stance and slipped his hands into his trouser pockets. When he shook his head, Angela got the impression the gesture was one of sadness. Finally he spoke, his words soft.

"Angela, obviously I can't tell you what to do. You're a consenting adult, and you have to make these kinds of decisions for yourself. But. . ." He lowered his gaze for a moment, taking in a deep breath. When he looked at her again, she sensed pain in his eyes. "But if you would just consider one question before you go back in there. If Jesus were sitting in the chair beside you, how comfortable would you be?"

It was the last thing she expected him to ask. "I—I never

thought of it that way. . . ." Would she be comfortable drinking beer if Jesus were sitting at the table? She examined herself and realized she wouldn't feel at ease if that were the case. Shame returned, sitting like a stone in her belly. Aunt Eileen had told her Jesus would help her resist temptation. Why hadn't she given Him the opportunity to help her?

"It's not that I want to be around beer. Funny"—she wrinkled her nose—"it doesn't even smell good to me anymore." She held out her hands in inquiry. "But what am I supposed to do? They're my friends. Should I tell them they can't have it when I'm around?"

Ben shrugged. "As I said, I can't tell you what to do, only what I would do. And I wouldn't put myself in a position of temptation. Plus, there's a biblical warning about being a stumbling block to other believers. Others, just seeing you there, might be given the impression you think drinking is okay. Is that a message you want to convey?"

Angela's chest constricted. Being at the table with her friends had convinced Ben she thought drinking was accept-able. Did she want others to get that impression of her? She looked at him, ready to tell him how sorry she was, but he spoke first.

"If those people in there are your real friends, Angela, they won't try to tempt you to do something you don't want to do." The earlier disapproval returned in his eyes and his tone, causing a cold band to clamp around her heart. "They'll respect the change in your lifestyle. If they can't do that. . ." His voice drifted off, but Angela knew the end to the sentence.

She released a big sigh. "I didn't know being a Christian would be so. . .hard."

A tiny smile toyed at the corners of Ben's lips. "It's easier when you aren't by yourself." Angling his head to gesture toward the restaurant, he said, "Putting yourself in those kinds of situations is asking for trouble. The Bible warns us not to yield to temptation."

Angela remembered the urge she'd felt to snatch up that glistening mug and gulp the cold liquid. She nodded. "I know, but. . ." But she didn't know what else to say. There were no arguments that made sense, no words that would excuse her from knowingly doing wrong. Setting her mouth in a grim line, she stood silently before Ben, observing how the late evening sun threw shadows on his face. It made him appear stern and unapproachable.

"Well"—Ben pulled his hand from his pocket and jiggled his car keys—"I've got to go. Bible study at church. You. . .take care, Angela." He turned his back and strode quickly to his waiting pickup.

Angela remained at the edge of the asphalt, watching until Ben's truck pulled out of the parking stall and headed toward the street. She had two choices—leave or return to her friends. She thumped her head with the butt of her hand as she realized she'd left her purse under her chair. She'd need to retrieve it.

Stepping back into the restaurant, she took a breath of fortification before returning to the table. Instead of sliding into the seat, she reached under the chair for her purse, fully intending to grab it and run.

But Alex shot her a broad smile. "Hey! You're back! You were gone so long we thought you deserted us. Pizza's here. Better grab some before Todd eats it all."

Todd slapped a piece of sausage and mushroom onto Angela's plate. "Yeah. Come on, sweetheart. You came to eat, right?"

No other mention was made about the beer she'd left to

turn warm in the mug. The spicy smell of the pizza was tantalizing—she hadn't eaten since eleven thirty. She was hungry. Eating wouldn't hurt anything, right? The welcoming smiles of her friends lured her into her chair.

She picked up the pizza. As she took the first bite, she realized she hadn't asked God to bless the food. The rock of shame returned, filling her stomach so thoroughly she had a hard time swallowing the bite of pizza. She managed to choke down half of a piece while listening to the others laugh and joke. Some of the jokes made her ears burn. She contributed nothing to the conversation.

Sitting there, listening, she came to the realization that she no longer fit with this crowd. The camaraderie was gone. Why had she thought she could slip back into the old crowd and have things be like they used to be? She wasn't the same person. Her Bible told her she was a new creation. She needed to start acting like it.

Dropping the half-eaten slice of pizza onto her plate, Angela reached beneath her chair and picked up her purse. She opened her purse and withdrew a few bills. "Here." She handed the money to Janine. "For my part of the pizza. I—I've got to go."

"Hey!" Janine's eyes flew wide. "What's wrong? You sick?"

Angela shook her head. She wasn't sick, except maybe sick at heart. And Janine certainly wouldn't understand that. "No, but I can't stay. I attend church—Grace Chapel—and on Wednesday nights they have a Bible study. I'm going to miss it if I don't get going."

The two men hooted with laughter.

"Angela—at Bible study?" Todd slapped the table. "Now there's a joke!"

Alex roared, and Janine punched his shoulder to bring him under control.

Angela felt her cheeks fill with heat. Gathering her courage, she said, "It isn't a joke. It's important to me. And, for future reference, I—I'd like to be able to see you guys, but I can't—I won't—be doing any more partying. So if you want to go to a movie or something sometime—"

Todd cut in. "Yeah, kiddo. If a good G-rated cartoon comes to the theater, I'll give you a ring."

Janine giggled and Alex snorted. The three of them sent smirking grins at one another, enjoying their private joke.

Angela hung her head. Ben was right. These weren't her friends, or they wouldn't try to hurt her this way. Without saying good-bye, she turned and hurried from the restaurant.

twelve

Ben pulled into the parking lot of Grace Chapel, killed the engine, but then just sat behind the steering wheel, staring across the wheat fields that faced the church. Angela had gone back into the Ironstone. He'd seen her. After warning her, after encouraging her, she'd turned around and gone right back to a potentially dangerous situation.

Lord, I can't do this again. I can't watch someone else I love travel the road to addiction. . . .

He straightened in his seat as the reality of his prayer struck him. He loved Angela. And more than just as a sister in Christ. Somehow his employer to employee, mentor to mentee relationship had developed into a man-to-woman relationship. But shouldn't the realization that he had fallen in love be a happy one? He didn't feel happy. He felt burdened. And betrayed.

How could God allow him to give his heart to someone so risky? Kent's face appeared in his memory—not the healthy Kent, but Kent-after-drug-overdose. Loving Kent had been risky, too. But, he argued with himself, loving Kent while he made his horrible choices was different. They'd had a relationship that went back to their babyhood.

But Angela? There was no long-standing relationship, no storehouse of memories years in the making. *Of course I should continue to love Kent. He is my childhood best friend and lifelong cousin. But*—he popped the door open and stepped out—*I cannot invest that much of myself in Angela. It hurts too much.*

As he strode across the parking lot, he sent up another prayer. *Let me love her with Christian concern for a fellow believer, but take the other love out of my heart, God.* He slipped into a folding chair on the outside aisle, closing down thoughts of Angela to concentrate on the Bible study.

The minister announced the passage for the evening's study, then began reading from Genesis 6—God's directions to Noah on the building of the ark. Ben listened, his brows pulled down, wondering what Pastor Joe had in mind.

When he read his closing verse from chapter 7, suddenly Ben understood. " 'And Noah did all that the Lord commanded him.' " A smile tugged at Ben's cheeks as the minister faced the gathered worshippers and asked, "Has God ever commanded you to do something that made no sense?"

Loving Angela made no sense. It promised to get him hurt. He was doing it anyway. But was it something God had designed, or was it just his own heart's desire?

"Think about how Noah must have felt, being told to build a three-story boat—nowhere near a body of water, but right in the middle of the desert—and then fill it with animals because rain was going to flood the earth." Pastor Joe released a light laugh. "I have to tell you, if I'd been Noah, I probably would have been rolling on the sand, holding my stomach, and laughing hysterically. It made no sense!

"Many Bible scholars believe the concept of rain was new. That the earth was like a huge terrarium, with a perfect balance of moisture. If that's true, then the idea of rain falling from the sky was unheard-of and would have been completely incomprehensible to Noah's way of thinking."

He chuckled softly. "I can imagine Noah scratching his head, trying to make sense of these commands of God. Build a boat, one three stories high, right here on the sand. Fill the boat with the male and female of every kind of animal from four-legged beasts to winged creatures to those that creep upon the ground—a daunting task! Watch the sky because clouds will form and dump water enough to flood the entire earth.

"How many questions must have filled Noah's head! Did he ask these questions?" He consulted his Bible, shaking his head. "We don't know. But"—he lifted one finger—"what does that last verse I read tell us? Read it with me. . . ."

A chorus of, "And Noah did all that the Lord commanded him" echoed through the room.

Pastor Joe continued, sharing the importance of trusting God to know what's best even when it doesn't make sense to the human mind. Ben listened, but at the same time his thoughts raced, trying to balance his feelings for Angela with what God would command him to do.

"Pray for her."

Yes, Lord, I know I should pray for her. And he had been—regularly.

"Pray for her now."

The urge was too strong to ignore. Closing his eyes, Ben set aside the sound of the minister's voice and began to pray.

☙

Angela parked her car, opened the door, and swung her feet to the asphalt. But then she sat motionless, half in and half out of the car, debating with herself. When she'd left the pizza restaurant, her feelings were so battered she planned to skip the Bible study and just go to Aunt Eileen's apartment to lick her wounds. Yet, as she'd turned toward Elmwood Towers, something had tugged her heart toward the church.

Now, sitting in the parking lot, aware the study had started at least ten minutes ago, she felt reluctant to disrupt the service by entering late. She lifted her feet, ready to pull them into the car and head to the apartment after all, but that mysterious tug returned.

"Okay, okay!" she mumbled, snatching up her purse and Bible and pulling herself from the car. "I guess if I make a fool of myself walking in late, it's no worse than the fool I've made of myself already at the Ironstone."

She stepped through the church door then closed it as quietly as she could. On tiptoe, she made her way to the sanctuary. Scanning the room, she discovered a spattering of open seats, most of which were toward the front. No seats on the back row were open. She cringed. She did not want to walk in front of anyone and make a spectacle of herself.

Then she spotted several metal chairs, still folded, leaning against the wall near the doorway. Balancing her purse and Bible in one hand, she crept to the chairs and lifted one by the underside of the backrest. She carried it to the far end of the back row and managed to set it up behind the other chairs with a minimum of noise. A couple of people turned to look, but both smiled in a welcoming manner. She smiled back, the tension in her shoulders lessening.

The chair creaked slightly as she settled her weight into it, but she kept her gaze forward, focused on the minister, and hoped no one else noticed the sound. From what she could glean from coming in midstride, the topic this evening was following what God asks.

How appropriate. She listened, absorbing the words of the minister as he talked about Noah and his neighbors.

"You see, Noah's neighbors were wicked people. So wicked

that God saw no reason to allow them to continue in sin. The Bible doesn't tell us how they reacted to the sight of that huge boat growing in the sand, but if they were ungodly, wicked people, we can surmise they probably gave Noah a hard time. Maybe called him names, asked him if he'd lost his mind."

The minister leaned on the podium and pointed at the listening congregants. "How many of you welcome that kind of treatment?"

Angela shook her head. She'd just experienced it. She didn't like it at all.

"How do you think Noah reacted?"

His expectant face encouraged responses, and several people contributed their thoughts. Angela listened to all of them, but she liked the one delivered in a familiar voice—Ben's—the best.

"I think he turned a deaf ear to his neighbors and only listened to God's voice. How else could he have continued working on the ark for the number of years it must have taken without giving in to the taunting of the crowd and putting his hammer away?"

The minister must have liked Ben's response, too, because he nodded and smiled in Ben's direction. "That's a good point. When the voices of 'the world' surround us, it can be very easy to give in to them, to allow them to influence us. But if we close them out by focusing on the still, small voice of God, we can be assured of walking the pathway God has chosen for us." He paused for a moment, his face pursing in sadness. "I wonder how many people miss a tremendous blessing because they allow themselves to be pulled off course by the tauntings of an ungodly crowd."

Angela remembered her impulse to return to the apartment

this evening as a result of her friends' teasing. She would have missed this lesson and the resulting blessing if she had followed through on that impulse. Gratitude washed over her. *Thank You, Lord, for tugging me here.*

"Now," the minister continued, as Angela leaned forward, eager to hear more, "how do you think Noah was able to do all that God commanded him without getting off course?"

A lady near the front raised her hand. "Noah had a long relationship with God. The Bible says his father also walked with God, so surely Noah had seen faith in action by watching his father."

Angela's heart flip-flopped. She'd not had such influences while growing up. Would that stymie her ability to follow God unconditionally?

"And," the woman went on, "he'd taught his sons to follow God, too."

"What makes you think that?"

Angela could tell by the pastor's tone his question wasn't a challenge but an invitation for the woman to share her thoughts.

"Because God told Noah he could bring his sons onto the ark. I think that means God recognized Noah had passed on the tradition of trust in God to his children."

The pastor gave a thoughtful nod. "Interesting. . . And what that means, if I'm following your train of thought correctly, is Noah had a built-in support system of people who would encourage him to continue work on the ark even if the townspeople proclaimed it a foolish waste of time."

The woman's head bobbed up and down in agreement.

Turning his attention to the entire congregation, the minister said, "This brings up a good point. We should be strong enough to stand alone if need be. The Holy Spirit can give us the strength to do that, when we ask. Yet how much more secure we feel when we have a body of believers standing behind us.

"Noah had his wife, his sons, and his sons' wives assisting in his efforts. God could have given Noah the strength and ability to do all of the tasks necessary to build the ark and gather the animals on his own, but God allowed Noah's family to contribute." Tipping his head, he raised his eyebrows. "Perhaps we can take a lesson from this and add that God wants us to have the support and assistance of other believers."

Angela hung her head, tears stinging her eyes. The support and assistance of other believers. . . Those words echoed through her head. Who did she have? Her list in the tablet at home was alarmingly short.

And how would the list grow? She didn't know how to lengthen it. The last name on the list was Ben's, and as much as she wanted him to be a part of her support system, it seemed he found fault with everything she did. Her past mistakes had put a huge barrier between them. Now, because of what she'd done long before she met him, he didn't trust her with Kent, and he didn't trust her to be with her old friends.

If she tried to form a relationship with other Christian people, would they react the same way as Ben had when they learned about the foolish things she'd done? Would they be able to look beyond the old Angela to the Angela she was trying to be with God's help? How she wanted a support system of believers, but she didn't think she could take being turned away time and again when others learned about her past mistakes.

God, I want a support system of believers. I need help right now. People who will pray for me and help me grow in You.

Pastor Joe brought the study to an end with a gentle admonishment to trust God to know what's best even if it doesn't make sense. "God's ways aren't our ways, and He sees what is waiting around the bend even when we can't. Let us walk in faith on the pathway He directs, trusting it will always be in our best interests."

He mentioned the prayer needs of the church membership, welcomed a few more requests from the attendees, and then dismissed the people to gather in small groups for prayer. Angela watched as some people rose and left the sanctuary and others shifted their chairs to create groupings. Her heart pounded with the desire to join one of those groups, to be a part of praying.

She glanced around the room, seeking Ben—he would at least be one familiar face. But then she saw him again in her memory, his disapproving frown, and she heard his admonishing words. Joining Ben's group would be a mistake. Why set herself up for more rejection?

So she remained in the corner, separated from the others. Loneliness smashed down on her, bringing the sting of tears. Lowering her head, she closed her eyes. Even if she wasn't part of a group, she could still pray. She sorted through the requests mentioned by the minister, lifting them one by one to the heavenly Father. And when she'd completed the list, her thoughts returned to her own needs.

Dear Lord, I need. . .friends. People like Noah had with his family, people to support me and help me in the task You've given me. Please, Father, won't You bring some friends into my life?

Her prayer was interrupted by the touch of a hand on her shoulder. Her heart leapt in hopefulness. Ben?

thirteen

Angela's eyes popped open and she raised her head, a smile forming on her face without conscious thought. The smile wavered when she found not Ben but Pastor Joe standing beside her chair. She pushed the disappointment aside and greeted the man in a whisper.

"Hello. I—I enjoyed the study this evening."

Pastor Joe grabbed a chair and slid it across the linoleum floor. He placed it next to her then sat down, his gentle smile lighting his eyes. "I'm glad you enjoyed it." He kept his voice low, too. "It's good to see you here on a Wednesday evening. I hope you'll make our Bible study a regular part of your week."

She nodded, eagerness filling her. "I'd like that. I know I have a lot to learn."

The pastor smiled. "Is there a prayer need I can address for you?"

He had a kind face, and Angela found herself feeling very at ease with him. *Surely a minister won't turn away from me if I share my failings, will he?* She searched his face and, seeing only interest, found the courage to share her deepest secrets.

"Yes. There is." She swallowed the nervous giggle that tried to find its way from her throat. "And it's a biggee."

The minister laughed softly. "There's nothing too big for God. What is it?"

"I need friends." Blurted out that way, it sounded childish. And selfish. Thinking about the other requests—a sister who fought cancer, a man who lost his job, a family whose house was destroyed in a fire—Angela felt heat climb her cheeks at her own audacity in requesting prayer for something so frivolous.

But the minister didn't even blink. "You don't have friends?"

Angela grimaced. "Well, I do. . .kind of." She took a deep breath. "You see, four months ago I had a huge circle of friends. They're still out there, but I don't feel like I can be with them anymore. With those friends, I started using drugs. Then I provided drugs for a party. I got caught, and a judge gave me a one-year sentence. I spent the first two months of the sentence in drug rehab, and now I'm serving the remainder in community service."

Pastor Joe simply nodded. His gentle face showed no shocked recrimination.

Grateful for his acceptance, Angela plunged on. "I became a Christian while I was in drug rehab, and I really want to do things right now. I don't want to mess up. But I haven't found very many people who are Christians who want to be my friend. The drug thing. . ." She sighed, Ben's face once more appearing in her memory. "Well, it gets in the way. And I can't be with my old friends because they still do things I shouldn't be doing now that I'm a Christian. So. . ." She held her hands out in a gesture of futility. "I'm. . .alone."

Leaning forward, the minister rested his elbows on his knees. His relaxed position helped Angela set aside the remainder of her worries about rejection. "First of all, let me assure you of one thing—you aren't alone. Ever."

Angela nodded. Aunt Eileen had told her the same thing.

"You have a built-in support system with the Holy Spirit, and He is an ever-present friend on whom you can depend.

But"—he smiled—"that having been said, I understand the need for earthly friends. Like-minded people of faith who will not only support you in your Christian walk, but who will also be there to hang out with, have fun with. Fellowship is important, too."

Angela nearly sagged with relief. He didn't think she was being silly! She leaned forward, eager to have her next question answered. "So how do I find these friends? My experience has been that some Christians are so put off by my past, they can't accept me today." It stabbed her heart to say the words, yet they were truthful. She desperately needed this man's advice.

The minister's face pulled into a slight scowl. "I'm sorry you've encountered judgmental attitudes. I understand why people react that way. Sin is difficult to face when you try so hard to avoid it. Yet Christ encourages us to look past the sin to the sinner, to love the sinner in spite of the sin." Tipping his head, he added, "Now, that doesn't mean we blithely accept the sin. We must caution those who walk in darkness that they're choosing an unhealthy pathway. We want to guide them to the light. But we must admonish in love. Do you understand the difference?"

Angela puckered her lips as she considered what he'd said. Was it possible Ben had tried to do what the minister mentioned? Admonish her in love? Perhaps his words weren't so much of condemnation, but of concern. Oh, she hoped so! Pastor Joe waited for a response. She believed she understood what he meant, so she nodded.

His gentle smile returned. "Angela, I believe you will discover many Christians are able to love the sinner in spite of the sin. Please don't dwell on those who have chosen to judge you. Forgive them for hurting you and move on. Also, use the experience to help you react kindly to those you encounter with less-than-perfect pasts. That way you're using the experience for good."

Angela hoped she would never make anyone feel as soiled as Ben—whether intentionally or unintentionally—had made her feel. She returned to her original question. "So where do I find these Christians who will be able to accept my past?"

"Well. . ." Pastor Joe sat up, raising his shoulders in a shrug. "As a matter of fact, we have something coming up that might be just what you're looking for. Wait here. I'll be right back." He rose and strode from the room while Angela waited, licking her lips in anticipation. When he returned, he handed her a folded brochure. "Our young adult singles are traveling to Camp Fellowship, near the Oklahoma border, for a three-day retreat over Labor Day weekend."

Angela examined the brochure while he continued.

"There will be Bible study classes, as well as activity periods with opportunities for small groups to gather and several large group functions. It's a weekend meant to grow young adults in their Christian walks, and also to bolster relationships among the attendees. It would be a way for you to get better acquainted with our young adults, and perhaps friendships can be formed that will continue after the retreat."

Angela's heart thumped in hopefulness. "Do you really think it would be okay for me to go? I mean, considering my past. . ."

The man took the brochure and seemed to examine it closely, his brows tugged down. When he looked at her, his eyes sparkled with mischief. "I saw nothing in there that says rehab graduates need not apply."

Despite herself, Angela laughed. "Okay. I'll fill this out

tonight and write a check. Thank you for telling me about it."

"You're welcome." Pastor Joe placed his hand on Angela's shoulder. "Angela, being a new Christian is tough. It's like a baby learning to walk—lots of stumbles and scrapes and bruises. But the more you pick yourself up, dust yourself off, and continue to try, the stronger your legs will grow. I'll be praying for you as you get your Christian feet under you."

His image became blurred as tears filled her eyes. His kindness touched her, easing the bruises Ben's censure and her friends' unkind treatment had left on her heart.

"Let's pray right now." He lowered his head, folded his hands, and began petitioning the Lord on Angela's behalf.

Angela listened, his words wrapping around her like a warm blanket, soothing her and assuring her God was listening. By the time he'd finished, she felt certain God had planned for her to attend tonight so she'd learn about the retreat weekend. She could hardly wait for Labor Day to arrive to see what friendships God would provide.

He ended his prayer with an amen then said, "Just drop the registration tear-off in the office on your way out." He rose. "And enjoy the retreat."

"I will. Thank you." Angela hurriedly filled out the registration form, wrote her check, and headed for the office.

ε

Ben lifted his head after completing his prayer and spotted Pastor Joe with Angela, their heads bent in prayer. Relief rushed through his chest. If Pastor Joe were to begin mentoring Angela, he could back off—be relieved of his self-imposed responsibility.

But what if it wasn't self-imposed? What if it was God's prompting that had made him want to reach out to Angela in the first place?

He pushed that thought aside. Surely God wouldn't expect him to go through the heartache of witnessing someone's descent into drug addiction. God loved him too much to put him in a position destined to bring him despair. It was better to allow Pastor Joe to assume mentoring with Angela. Pastor Joe was stronger, better equipped to deal with Angela's special needs.

Rising from his chair, he said good-bye to the members of his prayer group and promised to continue praying for their needs over the course of the week. The others offered their good-byes and moved toward the foyer area, but one member of the group, Stephanie, stopped Ben with a manicured hand on his arm.

"Ben, do you have any needs I can pray for this week?"

Ben looked into Stephanie's brown eyes. In the past, he'd gotten the impression that Stephanie would like more than a casual acquaintanceship, but he saw no hint of coquettishness in her expression. Deciding she was sincere, he nodded.

"As a matter of fact, there is. It's something related to. . ." He paused, uncertain how to phrase things to make sense without giving too much away. Then he realized he didn't need to give Stephanie the details. God knew the details. A simple request would be sufficient. "If you'd pray for God's will in a situation at my workplace, I would appreciate it."

Stephanie didn't pry—just offered a smile and a nod. "I'll certainly do that." Her fingers tightened on his arm. "And you be sure and keep me updated, will you? I always like hearing the praise reports."

Ben quirked one brow, grinning. "Oh, believe me, if there's reason to praise, you'll hear about it."

"Good." She removed her hand, but her bright smile invited further conversation.

"So did you sign up for the singles' retreat? I'm really looking forward to it. The speaker they've secured is supposed to be very good."

Ben had heard that, too. "Yes, I did sign up. And I'm glad you mentioned it, because I need to remember to put in a request for early leave on the Friday before Labor Day. My boss will need to cover the close-down duties that day."

They continued to visit, discussing the retreat and who all had signed up to go. Then the conversation lagged, and Stephanie glanced around the room. "Oh! I didn't realize we'd been chatting so long. Everyone else is gone."

Ben noticed, too, for the first time that no one else remained in the sanctuary. He hadn't even seen Angela leave. A feeling of regret niggled, but he pushed it aside with a light chuckle. "We'd better clear out. The custodian is probably eager to shut things down for the night."

"Yes." Stephanie fixed him with a sweet smile. "Would you like to go grab a cappuccino or something? Talk a little more?"

Ben groped for an adequate response. Part of him was tempted. Stephanie was attractive, and spending time with her would certainly help remove thoughts of Angela from his mind. Yet he realized accepting her invitation might give her the impression of interest in her, which didn't exist. He wouldn't use her to soothe his own concerns.

"It sounds like fun, Stephanie, but I need to get home. Maybe another time?" He softened the refusal with a smile.

She smiled, too, giving a shrug. To his relief, she didn't appear offended. "That's fine. It was just a thought. You take care, and I will be praying."

Ben walked her to her car and opened the door for her,

giving her another good-bye. Her warm smile, accompanied by a cute little fingers-only wave, made him swallow and back away. Why hadn't he noticed before how appealing Stephanie was?

He watched her vehicle pull away before climbing into his truck. As he drove toward home, his thoughts bounced back and forth between the two women with whom he'd conversed privately this evening.

Angela, with her autumn-colored hair and intriguing pale blue eyes.

Stephanie, with hair the color of a walnut shell and dark eyes to match.

Angela, who wore an expression of seeking.

Stephanie, who gave an aura of self-assurance.

Angela, with her questionable past.

Stephanie, with her sterling reputation.

If a person put them side by side in a beauty contest, Angela would certainly come out the winner. But as a potential life's mate? In that contest, Stephanie's attributes were certainly the preferable ones from a Christian viewpoint. Perhaps he would be wise to explore the opportunity of a deeper friendship with Stephanie.

His heart contracted painfully as Angela's image crowded out the one of the other woman. *Now, stop that!* he commanded himself. Hadn't he decided that a relationship with Angela was not beneficial to him? Caring for her only brought pain and misery. He'd traveled the pathway of destruction once before as an unwilling observer. He would not put himself in that position again, no matter how his heart raced every time she came near. He'd just have to set aside those feelings.

"Mind over matter," he reminded himself as he pulled into

the driveway of his fourplex. Surely if he distanced himself from Angela, he could forget her.

He shut off the ignition and froze for a moment. Forget her? Did he really believe that was the right thing to do? Lowering his head, he prayed, "God, please forgive me. Of course I don't want to forget Angela. You placed her needs on my heart. I made a promise to mentor her, to support her in prayer, and I will honor that promise. But, God, please. . .her past. . . She can't change it, and I can't seem to change how I feel about what she did. As long as the issue of her drug use is between us, there can't be anything more than a casual friendship. Help me see her in the way You would have me see her. Let me be her friend, her mentor, but please. . .guard my heart."

fourteen

Ben dropped the reports into their file and closed the drawer with a snap. He glanced at the clock and then shook his head at his own impatience. The anticipation was as bad as it had been when he was a kid planning to go to summer camp.

He admitted part of the anticipation had to do with the opportunity to distance himself from Angela for a few days. The past two weeks had been rough, and prayer had been his constant companion. As he'd promised, he prayed for her daily, for her to resist the temptation to fall back into drug use and for her to grow in her Christian walk. But he hadn't watched closely enough to see if his prayers were having any effect. Looking at Angela brought a rush of longing he wanted to squelch.

Rising from his desk, he scanned the area for Philip. Although he couldn't see Philip, he could hear him from behind the partition of the kitchen area, bantering with one of the clients. Ben crossed the room and ducked behind the partition as Angela crossed his path, leading two clients to the washroom to clean up after sorting recyclables. He released his breath in a whoosh, thankful for the chance to hide behind the tall partition and get his racing heartbeat back under control.

Ben waited until Philip gave the client a clap on the shoulder and turned away, signaling the end of their conversation, before speaking. "Philip? I just wanted to remind you—"

"That you're leaving early." Philip grinned. "I know, I know.

You've only told me twice already today." Shaking his head, he chuckled. "I'm beginning to think you really want to get away from here for a while."

Ben laughed, too, but he was certain he looked as sheepish as he felt. "It isn't the job. You know that."

Philip nodded. Ben had shared his confusion about his feelings for Angela with Philip and Philip's wife Marin. Both Philip and Marin were praying for the situation, for God's will to be made known.

Suddenly Philip frowned. "Odd, I just remembered. It seems Angela. . ." His voice trailed off as he passed Ben and headed around the corner, toward the break area.

Ben followed, puzzled.

Philip went to the check-in sheet hanging near the time clock, and he poked the pages with his finger. "I was right. Angela leaves early today, too."

Ben's heart turned a somersault. He broke out in a cold sweat. "Do you know why?"

Philip shrugged. "Something about weekend plans, and she needed to leave two hours early. I had to get it approved through the probation officer, and the approval came in yesterday, just under the wire. She was pretty relieved. Must be something important."

"Yeah, must be." Ben pinched his chin, thinking. When he and Stephanie had talked about those who had signed up for the weekend, Angela's name hadn't been mentioned. In all likelihood, she simply had plans for the long weekend just as he did. The plans didn't have to be for the same thing. Yet, as he tried to assure himself, doubt continued to gnaw at him.

He had to know. Although he hadn't spoken to her beyond casual greetings and farewells since he'd warned her in the parking lot at the Ironstone, he headed out of the break area and went looking for her. His heart pounded as he approached. It doubled its tempo when he tapped her shoulder and she turned, her face breaking into a smile.

"Ben. Did you need something?"

Unconsciously, his gaze swept across her rumpled hair. Those curls, as always, created a desire to run his hands through the shining locks. He cleared his throat. "Yes. Um. . . Philip mentioned you have plans to leave early today?"

She nodded, and then her face clouded. "I'm sorry. Should I have mentioned it to you, too? Philip didn't say anything when I asked him about it. . . ."

He shook his head. "No, no, clearing it with Philip was the right thing to do. He is the head honcho around here." Her smile returned, but it trembled around the edges, giving her a winsome expression. He stuck his hands in his pockets. "I just wondered if. . .well, if you had specific plans for the weekend?"

Her fine brows came down in puzzlement, and for a moment he thought she would refuse to answer. But then her expression cleared and she offered a graceful shrug. "Yes, my plans are quite specific. I'm going on a church retreat."

Ben's heart thudded against his ribs. "Church. . . As in Grace Chapel?"

Her eyebrows shot high. "Yes! Are you going, too?"

The anticipation melted away to be replaced by a heavy weight of dread. An entire weekend with Angela? Getting through the workdays had been excruciating. What would he do when she was there at breakfast, lunch, supper, and throughout the evening? *Maybe I should cancel my plans. . . .*

He instantly nixed that thought. He'd been looking forward

to this weekend for too long to abandon it now. "Yes. Yes, I'm going, too."

"Oh, wonderful! Pastor Joe said it would be a perfect time for me to formulate friendships. You said yourself I needed to make Christian friends instead of hanging out with my old crowd."

She seemed to search his face, and he got the impression she needed his approval. He managed a brief nod. "Yes, that's a great idea. With four different churches sending their singles to the camp this weekend, you should have several opportunities for building friendships." Now why did the thought of Angela forming relationships beyond him make his chest feel tight?

"That's what I'm hoping." She shook her head, making her curls dance. "But I've got a lot to finish up here before I can leave, so. . ."

He got the hint. "Sure. Finish up. I'll—I'll see you later."

He fled to his desk and sat down, fighting the urge to bury his face in his hands. "It's okay," he mumbled to himself as he punched the computer keys to open the budget log. "The campground is big. Lots of people. You'll hardly see her."

"You say something, Ben?"

Philip's curious voice brought Ben's head up.

"Huh?" He hadn't realized he'd spoken loud enough for anyone to hear. Shaking his head, he forced a grin. "No. No, just thinking aloud."

"Oh. Okay." Philip gave him a light pat on the shoulder. "Well, listen, if you need to leave now, I can look over the books."

Ben scooted his chair back and rose. "That'd be great. I do have some things I could do to get ready for the weekend."

Like pray for strength to make it through this weekend with Angela only a dormitory away.

"Fine." Philip plunked himself into Ben's chair. "See you Tuesday. And have a great weekend."

Ben yanked his car keys from his pocket. "Yeah, great. . ."

❧

Angela trotted to her car, her steps light and her heart singing. Ben had talked to her! After nearly two weeks of silence, he'd walked up, called her name, and talked to her. The joy that had washed over her in those moments still bubbled under the surface. How she had missed his companionship!

Her constant prayer had been for a restoration of their friendship. She knew she had disappointed him by meeting with Janine and the others at the Ironstone and having that beer on the table. But she'd been working so hard ever since to stay true to her Christian convictions and not do anything that would give anyone the impression that pleasing Jesus was not important to her.

Surely he'd noticed. That's why he'd spoken to her today. She couldn't stop the smile from growing on her face as she considered an entire weekend of activities with Ben. Pastor Joe had indicated the opportunity for building friendships existed. She mentally moved Ben to the top of her "support system" list.

She climbed into her vehicle, humming. Now that she knew Ben would be there, a feeling of security struck. As much as she had anticipated the weekend, an underlying nervousness had held back full-blown excitement. Being with strangers was never comfortable. But Ben's would be a familiar face, an island of recognition among a sea of strangers.

And with all the opportunities for interaction and joint activities, surely their friendship would grow. When they first met, she'd felt a spark. She longed for their relationship to be as it was before Ben knew about her drug use conviction. This weekend could prove to be a healing time for both of them. *Oh, please, Lord!* Her heart beat in hopeful double beats.

Since she had said good-bye to Aunt Eileen and put her bag in the car this morning before leaving for work, she drove straight to the church. Several other cars were already there, and two large vans waited by the sidewalk, the back doors yawning wide. People milled around the vans, some with bags in hand.

She parked her car with the others and got out, waving when a couple of people beside the vans waved at her. After retrieving her suitcase, she trotted to the vans. "Hi! Where do I put this?"

A dark-haired woman greeted her with a smile. "We ladies are going on the first van and the guys in the second, so you can put your suitcase in the back of the first one. Here, I'll take it." She took the suitcase from Angela then headed toward the first van. Peeking over her shoulder, she said, "I know I've seen you in Sunday school, but I've forgotten your name."

"I'm Angela." Angela trotted along beside her benefactor.

"And I'm Stephanie." Stephanie put Angela's suitcase with the others then held out her hand. "I'm glad you decided to join us."

Angela shook Stephanie's hand. "Thanks." She walked with Stephanie back to the milling group of women, her brain buzzing. Something about Stephanie was familiar, but she couldn't place it. She stayed in the group, learning everyone's name and chatting, while more cars pulled into the parking lot and the backs of the vans filled with suitcases.

Not until she saw Ben's pickup pull in did she remember where she'd seen Stephanie before. At Bible study two weeks ago, huddled in a corner with Ben. Jealousy smacked hard, and Angela felt her breath catch. Could it be that Ben had avoided her recently for more reasons than her past mistakes?

She watched him cross the parking lot, duffel bag in hand. He tossed his lumpy bag into the back of the last van, his T-shirt pulling taut with the swell of his muscles. When she glanced at Stephanie, she observed the other woman's gaze following Ben, too.

Lord, guard my actions. The prayer came automatically, a recognition of behavior that wasn't pleasing to her Savior. The simple prayer settled her ruffled feathers, and she took a big breath, managing to smile when Ben turned in their direction.

When his gaze fell on her, she saw his steps falter, his grin fade. Then he seemed to shift his gaze to Stephanie, and the smile returned. A pain stabbed through Angela's heart.

Her earlier hopes of establishing a closer friendship with Ben melted beneath the early September sun. Reality crashed around her, reminding her that someone like Ben—strong, steadfast Ben—would never be interested in someone whose past was so shaded.

When he stopped in front of Stephanie, Angela took a step backward, forcing a smile she didn't feel. "I—I'm going to get in the van now. See you all in a few minutes."

"Okay, Angela." Stephanie's bright smile did little to ease Angela's discomfort. "I'll join you in a minute or two."

Angela paused long enough to see Stephanie lift her smile to Ben's face; then she turned and fled to the van. Inside the vehicle, alone with her thoughts, she hunkered into the seat and closed her eyes tight, trying to shut away the image of Ben with Stephanie.

The two had looked right together—both with their long-time Christian lives. Who was she fooling, thinking she was worthy of someone like Ben? She fought tears as shame once again filled her chest, bringing a stifling weight of regret. She allowed herself a few minutes of mourning, of whining silently to God over being stuck in an emotional roller-coaster ride. And when she'd finished, she straightened in the seat and dashed away her tears with the insides of her wrists.

She would not spend this weekend moping. Pastor Joe had said she would find Christian friends who would accept her. So Ben didn't accept her. So what? Ben wasn't the only person who would be at the campground this weekend. There would be lots of other people. She'd just have to set her sights elsewhere. It was time to broaden her horizons, to stop looking at Ben as the only answer to her loneliness.

Lord, I've prayed for friendships. Pastor Joe has prayed for friendships for me, too. I trust You to meet that need this weekend. Thank You for the people You will bring into my life.

"Hi."

The greeting startled Angela out of her prayer. She jerked her gaze up to find a smiling young woman standing in the van's open doorway.

"Mind if I join you? I've been on my feet all morning, and I'm ready to sit down."

Angela scooted over and patted the seat. "Sure. By the way, I'm Angela."

"I'm Robyn."

"Nice to meet you."

Robyn grinned, dimples flashing. "You, too."

They began to chat, and thoughts of Ben thankfully slipped into the background as the groundwork was set for establishing a new friendship.

fifteen

Angela swung her suitcase and, with a grunt, managed to plunk it onto the mattress of an upper bunk.

Sitting on the bunk below, Robyn grinned. "Wow! I think we'll call you Muscles from now on!"

Angela looked at the other woman and laughed. Rubbing her shoulder, she said, "I don't think one lucky swing is enough to earn that title. And I hope I'll have enough room to sleep up there with the suitcase, because I'm not willing to wrestle it down until it's time to leave on Monday."

On the bunk next to Angela's, Stephanie stopped rolling out her sleeping bag and said, "If you sleep all coiled up like a roly-poly bug, you'll be fine with that suitcase on the end. Or you could stretch out and use it as a footrest."

Although Angela had tried her best to dislike the dark-haired woman—after all, she had Ben's attention—she just couldn't maintain the feeling. Stephanie was so sweet, Angela found herself drawn to her. On the drive over, with Robyn between them, Stephanie had repeatedly leaned forward and included Angela in conversation. Angela couldn't make herself rebuff Stephanie now.

Forcing a laugh, Angela said, "I think I'll have to sleep with my head on the suitcase. I just realized I brought sheets, but I didn't bring a pillow."

Stephanie picked up one of the plump pillows from her bed and tossed it over. "There you go, with my compliments."

Angela picked it up and hugged it. "Are you sure? You brought two. You must have intended to use them."

With a grin, Stephanie folded the remaining pillow in half, thumped it onto the mattress, and rested her head on it. "This'll work fine."

"Well, then. . .thanks." Angela swallowed the lump in her throat. It had been a long time since she'd been treated with such unconditional acceptance and kindness by virtual strangers.

Robyn bounced up from her mattress, her eyes sparkling behind the round lenses of her glasses. "Well, now that we're settled, let's head to the cafeteria. Supper starts in another fifteen minutes."

Several others were already heading for the door that led to the hallway. Angela, Stephanie, and Robyn fell in with them. The group laughed and talked as they made their way across a grassy courtyard that separated the dormitories from the main buildings. Angela found herself feeling at ease, and peacefulness washed over her. *Thank You, Lord, for bringing me here.*

Outside the cafeteria doors, a table was set up beneath a green canvas pavilion, and a smiling woman distributed plastic-sleeved name tags printed with each person's name and church of attendance. Each tag also had colored stickers in the upper left-hand corner.

Angela found her name tag and examined it. A blue cross with a yellow rose sticker at its base was on her tag. Robyn's tag had a rainbow in clouds instead of the cross, but she also had a yellow rose. A glance at Stephanie's tag showed a green cross and white daisy.

The three women clipped their tags to their shirtfronts then got in line to enter the cafeteria.

"I wonder what these are for." Angela wondered aloud, pointing to the stickers.

Robyn shrugged. "Decoration?"

A woman in line ahead of them turned around. Her name tag read: CHARLENE SCOTT, CALVARY CHURCH, SCOTT CITY, KS. She tapped her own symbols. Her flower sticker was a pink carnation. She also had a rainbow, but unlike Robyn's, hers had no clouds. "They'll use these to break us into groups. Sometimes they'll use one of the symbols, sometimes the color. It helps us get to know everyone who is here instead of staying in our own little groups."

Angela nodded and thanked her for the explanation. That made sense. And she liked the idea. The more people she could meet, the greater the opportunity to build her support system.

Once everyone had crowded inside the cafeteria, a man at the front of the room spoke into a microphone. "Welcome to Camp Fellowship, folks. We've got a great weekend planned for you, starting with our opening worship service right after supper. For the moment, check your name tags. We're going to make a seating assignment for tonight's meal."

A murmur went through the waiting crowd as people consulted their name tag stickers.

The man used the microphone to call out symbols while pointing out different areas in the cafeteria. Everyone moved to his or her directed location as the symbols were called. Angela smiled a good-bye to Robyn and followed Stephanie as she made her way through the crowd to the long tables indicated for those with cross symbols.

A couple of people squeezed between the two women, slowing Angela's steps, and she became separated from

Stephanie. Most of the chairs were filled by the time she reached the tables, but an end seat was open at the second table. She stood behind it then looked across the table.

Her heart seemed to forget its purpose when she realized Ben was right across from her. Their gazes met, and Ben's shoulders stiffened. For several long seconds they stared at each other, and Angela found herself wishing he would smile, engage in conversation, treat her the way he had before she had confessed her sinful past. But he remained silent while a bustle of activity continued around them.

"Shall we bow our heads for prayer?" asked the man with the microphone.

Relief welled when she could break eye contact with Ben. The man led the group in grace. Head bowed, Angela added a quick postscript to his prayer: *Let me have a good weekend of growth and friendship building, Lord, and if it's Your will, please let that friendship list include Ben.*

Chairs screeched on the painted concrete floor as the re-treaters seated themselves. Paper plates at each setting held sandwiches wrapped in aluminum foil, a cluster of green grapes, a small bag of chips, and a cup of pudding. Simple fare, but Angela didn't mind.

The man on her left tapped her shoulder. "Could you pass the mustard, please?"

"Sure." She picked up the bottle and handed it over.

The man smiled and glanced at her name tag. "Thanks, Angel."

Angela burst out laughing. Grabbing the corner of the tag, she angled it so he could read the whole thing. "That's Angela. I've never been called an angel before."

The man laughed, too, and Angela heard Ben's soft snort

from across the table. She refused to look at him and held out her hand to the man. "And you are?"

He took her hand, giving it a slight squeeze. His eyes were blue, although not as deep in color as Ben's. She liked the length of his blond hair, a little long over his collar and wavy across his forehead. He also had a dimpled smile, which he used to good advantage. "I'm Elliott. Great to meet you."

"You, too."

"I'm a member of Calvary Church in Scott City. How about you?"

Angela glanced at Ben. He held his sandwich in both hands, watching her over the top of the layers of wheat bread and ham. She turned back to Elliott. "I attend Grace Chapel in Petersburg. I'm not a member, though." Another quick glance at Ben. "Yet."

Ben turned his attention to his potato chips.

"So. . ." Elliott squirted his sandwich with mustard. "Have you ever been to one of these retreats before?"

Angela popped a grape in her mouth. "No, this is my first time. But I've been looking forward to it."

Elliott nodded. "Oh, you'll have a great time. These retreats are very well planned. The activities, the speaker, the music. . . And of course, The Course." He threw back his head and released an ominous *bwa-ha-ha-ha* that brought a round of laughter from the table.

Angela shook her head, her lips twitching with a smile. "And what does that mean—?" She imitated his menacing laugh perfectly.

His grin held approval. "Have you ever been someplace where they've had ropes courses set up?"

Chewing another grape, Angela shook her head. Her

curls tickled her cheek, and she pushed the hair behind her ear. "No."

Elliott glanced down the length of the table and raised his voice. "Hey, everyone! Who all has done the ropes course?"

Five people, including Ben, held up their hands. Ben was the closest person with a hand raised, and Elliott turned to him. "You want to tell her all about it?"

His gaze on his plate, Ben said, "Not particularly."

Angela felt color flood her face, and even Elliott paused for a moment, seeming put off by Ben's blunt reply. But he recovered quickly, gave a shrug, and turned back to Angela.

"Well, the most important thing you need to know is all the people who've done The Course are still here and breathing. In other words, they survived." He smirked. "And you will, too." He consulted her tag again. "Hm, blue cross, yellow rose. . ." He looked at his own tag. "Green cross, orange leaf." A pretend pout puckered his lips. "Well, Miss Angel, we probably won't be in the same group for the ropes course, but"—he winked—"I'll be sure to look you up and see how you liked it."

Angela laughed. "You be sure and do that. Hopefully I won't be the first person to not survive The Course."

As she turned back to her plate, she glimpsed Ben scowling at her. Suddenly he planted his hands against the edge of the table and pushed, his chair screeching against the floor. Without a word, he dropped his napkin beside his half-full plate and headed for the exit.

☙

Ben stepped outside the cafeteria and sucked in a big breath of evening air. The chatter of voices was filtered by the closed door, but the laughter and teasing could still be heard. He needed silence, privacy, solitude. A chance to convince himself that Angela's flirting with Elliott was no big deal. It would be a very long weekend if he allowed himself to get upset every time she talked to some other man. Half the people here were men, and someone as pretty as Angela would certainly garner attention. *And she sure knows how to respond to it!*

He stomped across the ground, jealousy filling his chest so fully he found it hard to draw a breath. A bench waited beneath a huge elm in the middle of the courtyard. He headed in that direction, determined to sit down and have a serious talk with himself about getting his feelings under control.

When he was halfway across the grass, someone called his name, and he nearly groaned. Spinning around, he spotted Angela trotting toward him, a determined look on her face. He folded his arms over his chest and waited for her to catch up.

"Yes? What do you need?" His tone was more brusque than he'd intended, but his fast-beating heart made breathing difficult.

She crossed her arms, too, and fixed him with a stern glare. "Well, if you really want to know, I need you to stop treating me like I've got leprosy. Truly, is it too much to ask for you to be civil?"

Ben scowled. "I am civil."

She huffed. "Then you and I are using different dictionaries. Civil means—"

"I know what civil means!"

"—polite." She raised her voice, tipping forward and lifting her chin defiantly. "It means being polite, and you were not polite in there. Not to me, and not to Elliott." Releasing a huge sigh, she shook her head, her tousled curls teasing her shoulders. "Ben, I'm sorry if my being here upsets you, but—"

"I'm not upset that you're here," he said, dropping his cross-armed pose and moving toward the bench.

She followed, hovering just behind his elbow. "Then why the gruff reply to Elliott's question? Would it have really hurt you to tell me about the course?"

He spun around again. "Do you want to know about the course? Okay, I'll tell you. They have a system of ropes and pulleys attached to tree branches, and—"

"Ben!" She clutched her temples, those autumn-colored waves covering her fingers.

Once more, his hands itched to capture the curls. He plunked his hindquarters on the bench and curled his fingers around the wooden edge of the seat. "What?"

Standing in front of him, she sighed again. Lowering her hands, she wove her fingers together and pressed her hands against her stomach. "The course isn't important." Her tone turned soft, imploring. "What's important is how we're going to get through three days together here if you are so uncomfortable with it."

Uncomfortable is an understatement, Ben thought wryly. The pressure in his chest became unbearable as he forced himself to breathe evenly. "Listen, Angela, it's just. . ." He pressed his lips together tightly for a moment, battling with himself. Honesty was needed here, but he didn't want to crush her. *Lord, please help me out here.*

"It's just what?" She took a step closer, her intriguing light-colored eyes begging him to explain.

Finally he blurted out, "Every time I look at you, I see you in a hospital bed, tubes sticking out everywhere, just like Kent after his overdose."

Her eyes widened and she jerked, as if his words had impaled her. "Ben, I told you, I don't use drugs anymore. That isn't going to happen to me."

"But I can't be sure!" He drew his hand down his face. "Do you know how many times I heard Kent say 'I won't do it anymore, Benny, I promise' Then days later, or weeks later, or months later I'd get a call—his mother, begging for help because Kent was at it again. I couldn't trust Kent when he said he'd stay clean, and I can't trust you!"

Tears welled in Angela's eyes, making the darker rim of her irises brighten.

Ben turned away, the sight of those tears creating a stab of pain in his heart. He didn't want to hurt her, yet he had to be honest. His gaze aimed across the campground to the grove of trees at the edge of the property, he finished, "Watching my cousin battle his addiction was the hardest thing I've ever faced. And then, that last time, when he nearly died. . ." He closed his eyes for a moment, grimacing with the remembered pain. "And now, seeing him in a wheelchair, knowing he will never be the same because of the drugs. . ."

"But, Ben." She touched his shoulder, her fingertips quivering. "I've told you and told you. I'm finished with drugs. I'll never use them again. I promise you that. Why can't you believe me?"

He jerked away from her touch, his shoulder tingling where her fingers had brushed. "I can't believe you because I've seen the stranglehold of drugs! Kent was a strong man, but he couldn't resist them. You—you're. . ." To his frustration, words failed. He leaped to his feet, facing her. "I can't do it again, Angela. I won't do it again. I will not watch someone else I love fight a losing battle against drug addiction." Pointing at her, he grated, "So I'm going to keep my distance, and you've got to help. Stay away from me, Angela. Please, just. . .stay away."

The tears broke free of their perch on her thick lashes and trailed down her cheeks. Ben released a muffled moan and spun from the evidence of her distress. A distress he'd caused. He brushed past her and charged to his dorm room. Shutting himself in the quiet room, he sank onto the edge of his bed and buried his face in his hands.

Lord, I didn't want to hurt her. Forgive me for hurting her, but I can't go through it again. I wish I'd never come here.

sixteen

Angela watched Ben storm across the grass toward the dormitories. Tears rained down her cheeks, but she made no sound. Her chest ached with the effort of containing her misery, yet she wouldn't give him the satisfaction of reducing her to sobs.

He loved her. She'd heard him say he couldn't watch someone else he loved fight a losing battle against drug addiction. He loved her, but he didn't trust her. She couldn't understand love like that. Shouldn't love and trust be synonymous?

As she stood beside the bench, a flutter of activity captured her attention. People spilled out of the cafeteria, moving en masse toward the worship hall. She should go, too, but her feet remained stubbornly still. Two people separated themselves from the throng and jogged across the grass toward her. Stephanie and Robyn.

Turning her back, Angela wiped away her tears with trembling fingers. Just as she turned around again, the pair came to a halt a couple of feet away from her. Their smiles faded when they looked into her face.

"Hey." Stephanie stepped forward and touched Angela's shoulder. "What's the matter?"

Robyn moved closer to put her arm around Angela. "I saw you charge out of the cafeteria after Ben. Is everything okay?"

Angela shook her head. "No. Everything is most definitely not okay. I need to go back to Petersburg. Is there any way I can get a taxi to come out here or something?"

Robyn and Stephanie exchanged looks. Stephanie spoke. "Angela, a taxi all the way back to Petersburg would cost you an arm and a leg. Come here." She guided Angela to the bench and gently pushed her onto the seat. She and Robyn squeezed in on either side of her. "Now tell us what's going on. Maybe we can help."

Angela looked from woman to woman. Even in the muted light from electric lamps at the top of poles, she could see the genuine concern on their faces. She had prayed for friends. Had God sent Stephanie and Robyn to fill that need? With a deep sigh, she sent up a silent prayer for their understanding then forged ahead.

"The problem is, I did something, several months ago, before I became a Christian. Ben knows about it, and it's. . ." She swallowed. "It's causing big problems."

Robyn put her hand on Angela's knee. "Do you mind telling us what you did?"

"I used drugs." She blurted the words out then searched their faces for their reactions. Neither pulled away or showed shocked disapproval. Relief flooded her, and she gained the courage to tell everything. She left out no details then finished with, "I'm a Christian now, and I've promised God I'll never use drugs again. But Ben doesn't believe me. He—he said he loves me." She glanced at Stephanie, fearful of hurting the other woman's feelings. "But he doesn't trust me. Not at all. And he asked me to stay away from him. That's why I've got to go back to Petersburg. I saw his name tag. He has a blue cross, too. I won't be able to stay away from him."

The trio sat in silence for several minutes. A frog croaked somewhere in the distance, and the breeze rustled the drying leaves overhead. From the sanctuary, a piano began to play, and voices answered the accompaniment. The gentle sounds of the evening wrapped around Angela, enveloping her in peace. She had shared her deepest hurt, her worst sins, and these two women hadn't gotten up to walk away. They remained, their presence a breath of Jesus to Angela's aching heart.

Finally Stephanie spoke. "I don't know how well Robyn knows Ben, but he and I were on a committee together last year at church. My impression of him is that he's very devoted to his faith." Putting her arm around Angela's shoulder, she offered a one-armed hug. "I'm sorry he hurt you. I would imagine he's hurting, too, and his pain is making him behave in ways not typical."

Angela wanted to believe that, but his withdrawal had been so complete after her confession of drug abuse. She sighed. "So what do I do? Do I stay or do I go?"

"Well, you don't go!" Robyn shifted slightly on the bench, her knees banging into Angela's. "We've just barely gotten acquainted! And I'd like to get to know you better."

"You would? Even after I told you—"

"What's past is past," Robyn said, her voice firm. "No one's perfect, Angela. We've all made mistakes, and in God's eyes, sin is sin. There aren't various levels, with one sin being worse than another. Sin is just. . .wrong. And my judging you for something you did before you became saved would be just as wrong as you continuing to use drugs now that your body is a temple for the Holy Spirit."

Gratitude welled up in Angela's heart and spilled over, bringing a fresh rush of tears. "Then you'll still be my friends?"

"Of course we will!" Robyn and Stephanie chorused together then giggled.

"Still, maybe it would be better if I left. Ben—" Angela started.

"Ben has to answer for Ben," Robyn inserted.

"I agree," Stephanie added. "Ben wanting to keep his distance is Ben's problem, not yours. And to be honest, his problem isn't going to be solved by you leaving. That will just make it easier for him not to face it. No, I think you should stay, enjoy the weekend, and let Ben solve this for himself. If he isn't comfortable around you, then he can make the decision to leave."

Angela looked back and forth, her heart swelling. God had answered her prayer already. True friends! Only true friends would be this supportive. Tears distorted her vision, but she blinked, sending them away. Slapping her own knees, she said, "All right then. I won't run away. But. . ." She bit down on her lower lip. "Could we pray about it? Because it's going to be very tough for me to face him in these group activities with this issue between us."

"Of course." Stephanie took one of Angela's hands then stretched the other hand toward Robyn. Robyn took Angela's free hand, completing the circle. The three lowered their heads and asked God to work His miracle in restoring peace for both Ben and Angela.

࿇

"You'll be okay, Angela." Bruce, the camp activities' director, shielded his eyes with his broad palm as he peered upward at Angela. "The rigging is secure, and I'm acting as anchor. I outweigh you by at least. . .oh, ten pounds."

Angela giggled from the square wooden platform in the tree branches a good twenty feet from the ground. Stocky Bruce outweighed her by at least a hundred pounds, but she appreciated his humor. Her heart pounded so hard, she was certain it would burst from her chest.

"And of course we've got muscleman Ben holding the other rope, so you've got nothing to worry about."

Angela glanced from Bruce to Ben. Ben didn't look at her, but she saw the whiteness of his knuckles as he gripped the taut rope. No matter his feelings toward her, he wouldn't let her fall. She knew that.

"So. . .are you ready?"

Angela looked ahead to the next tree. The ropes course led through six trees, weaving between branches, always well above the ground. She patted the sturdy straps of the rappelling rigging and drew in a breath of fortification. "I'm ready!"

"All right then. . .let go!"

Squeezing her eyes tight, Angela released the branch and coiled her fists around the thick shoulder straps of the rappelling gear. She felt herself whiz through the air, and an involuntary shriek left her lips.

"Open your eyes!" a female voice from the ground encouraged.

Angela peeked one eye open in time to see the rush of branches coming at her. She released another yelp as her feet connected with the second platform. Grabbing hold of a branch, she panted, blood rushing to her head.

The group on the ground applauded. "Woohoo, Angela! One down!"

Angela laughed and made a shaky bow from the platform. Those with blue crosses on their name tags laughed at her theatrics.

"See? Nothing to it!" Bruce hollered. "Ready to go again?"

Angela held her breath and gave a nod. She forced her eyes to remain open this time, and the exhilaration of the ride expressed itself in a burst of high-pitched laughter. Her feet on the third platform, she exulted, "Oh, this is fun!"

Laughter rose from the group. She glanced at Ben. A grin twitched his cheeks. Her own smile grew with the small signal of his pleasure.

"Then let's keep going," Bruce called. "No stops at platform four, just straight on to five, okay?"

"Okay!"

Angela finished the course, her heart racing, but not from fear. Bruce had explained the purpose of the ropes course was to practice letting go and letting God keep a person secure in an insecure world. Sailing through the air, depending on Bruce and Ben to keep her safe from falling, Angela experienced in a tangible way the upholding hand of God. *I trust You, Father, to never let me fall back into the habit of drug use ever again,* her heart promised as she allowed Ben and Bruce to lower her to the ground.

The moment her feet touched the leaf-scattered grass, the blue-cross group rushed forward, patting her back and offering congratulations. She sent smiles through the group, but as she turned, she caught a glimpse of Ben standing well back, his face impassive.

Her heart lurched, her elation faltering. But then she squared her shoulders and made another silent promise. *I won't let Ben's attitude defeat me, Lord. You are all I need for happiness. Thank You for never letting me down.*

❧

Ben looked across the bonfire to Angela, who sat between Stephanie and Elliott. The man had been like a leech during every free period today. But, he acknowledged, Angela hadn't given him any extra attention. Her flirtatiousness seemed to have been put on hold for the weekend.

Now she held a stick with marshmallows attached over the flame, turning it with a look of concentration on her face. The firelight danced on her tousled curls, bringing out highlights of gold and red. The shadows emphasized the delicate curve of her jaw and the height of her cheekbones. In the flare of the fire, her eyes took on a new luminance, as if lit from within. His heart lurched. Her beauty was like a knife through his chest.

He stifled a groan. This day had been so difficult. Their common symbol put them in nearly every activity together, making separation impossible. Despite his efforts to focus elsewhere, time and again his gaze had followed her. Images from the day replayed like slides on a private movie screen: Angela listening with rapt attention to the speaker, her head bent in silent prayer during quiet time, her elation as she ended the ropes course. And now, her sweet face tipped toward Elliott while fire glow lit her features.

Turning away, he tried to involve himself in conversation with the people sitting nearby, but he couldn't concentrate enough to contribute. With a sigh, he looked back across the flames, his eyes unconsciously seeking the cause of his conflict.

But she wasn't there.

He gave a startled jerk, sitting up straight and searching the area. The only light came from the massive bonfire, so he nearly missed the shadowy figure slipping between trees at the edge of the clearing. Had it not been for the flash of fire in her spiraling curls, he might not have recognized the figure as Angela.

Planting his palms against the log that served as his seat, he nearly lunged to his feet. But Bruce stepped in front of Ben, stopping his movement.

"Hey, gang, anyone have a suggestion?" Bruce patted the guitar that hung around his neck. "Let's sing some praise songs, give God the glory for providing such a beautiful fall evening."

Song suggestions were thrown out, and Bruce strummed, accompanying the voices. Ben sang along, but his participation was halfhearted at best. His gaze remained on the spot where he'd seen Angela disappear. Half an hour slipped by, and still she hadn't returned. Worry pressed at him. Could she have gotten lost? The campground was fairly large, and in the dark, in the trees, a person could get disoriented.

Leaning to the person seated next to him, he asked, "Hey? Do you know if anyone has a flashlight out here?"

The man nodded. "Yeah. Bruce's wife, Lorraine, brought a few of them in case people needed to get back to the dorms."

"Thanks." Ben rose and made his way to the back of the gathered campers to Lorraine. She willingly reached into a burlap bag and withdrew a flashlight at Ben's request. After thanking her, he circled around the group, moving cautiously over the shadowed ground.

He waited until he was in the trees before turning on the flashlight. The beam shot ahead no more than five or six feet, but it was enough to guide his progress. Watching the play of light on tree trunks and on the uneven, leaf-covered ground, Ben thought of the Bible verse in Psalms about God's Word being a lamp for man's feet and a light for man's path. The light only uncovered a path a few feet ahead—far enough to take three or four steps—but limited the vision of the entire path. He had to trust that the beam would continue shining as he made his progress, giving him enough light to continue.

God, it's like that in life, too, isn't it? You don't allow us to see the whole pathway, but You provide the illumination needed to make today's progress. His throat convulsed. *I don't know what lies ahead for Angela and me, but I want to trust that You have good things in store at the end of the road. Please let Your light keep shining. . .for both of us.*

A voice startled him, bringing his prayer to a close. He froze, straining to listen. At first he couldn't make out words, only tones; but then the voice raised, and he recognized not only the speech but also the speaker.

"Give that to me right now!"

Angela, making a demand.

Mumbled voices answered. Their words were unclear, but the growling tones indicated anger.

Ben stumbled forward, his heart pounding. The bouncing beam of the flashlight turned the trees into lunging monsters, but he kept going, determined to find Angela and protect her from—what? He didn't know. He only knew he had to get to her quickly.

The voices grew louder, an obvious argument ensuing. He let the sound guide him, his heart pounding harder with each step that brought him closer. He burst through several scrub bushes into a small clearing where a minuscule campfire sent out a weak flicker of light. Angela stood on one side of the fire; three people faced her from the other side. All four jumped and spun toward him as he charged onto the scene.

"What's going on here?" Ben swung the beam of the flashlight across the row of faces opposite Angela. He didn't know any of them. They were young, teenagers probably.

When they spotted Ben, one hollered, "Let's go!" They took off through the trees.

Ben started after them but changed his mind. He didn't care about those boys. He'd come out here for Angela. Turning back, he saw her trot around the campfire and bend down to pick something up. The flashlight aimed at her, he approached, his brows crunched. "What is that?"

She held it against her side for a moment, her face pale. Slowly she raised her hand, and Ben angled the flashlight beam on a plastic-wrapped bunch of crumpled brown leaves. Marijuana. *Oh, Lord, no. . .*

He lifted his gaze from the packet to her face. Her wide eyes told everything he needed to know. He'd interrupted a drug deal.

"Angela. . ." He shook his head, the disappointment sagging his shoulders. "How could you?"

seventeen

Angela took a stumbling step forward. The look of betrayal on his shadowed face stabbed her heart. "Ben! It isn't what you think!"

"What am I supposed to think?" he grated, his teeth clenched. "I come out here, worried about you, and I find you—I find you. . ." He released a groan.

She grabbed his arm. "Ben, I didn't come out here looking for drugs. I was just walking, thinking, trying to make sense of you and—" She stopped. There was no "you and me" where Ben and she were concerned. Drawing in a breath, she continued. "I saw the campfire, and I wondered who was here. I found those boys getting ready to make joints."

"So you decided to join them."

How his words stung! "No! Ben, listen to me. When I saw what they were doing, I tried to stop them."

Ben jerked his arm free, his gaze accusing. "I heard you asking for the marijuana, Angela. I heard you."

"Yes, I asked for it!"

"Well, if you weren't planning to use it, why did you ask them to give some to you?"

Frustration welled. How could she make him understand? "I didn't want them using it, making the same mistake I did, so I asked for it. Not for my use, but just to take it away! Ben, you have to believe me!"

But he shook his head, backing away from her. "Once a drug

user, always a drug user. You just couldn't stay away from it."

His withdrawal hurt worse than anything she'd experienced before. Her chin quivered with the effort of holding back tears. What had she decided about Janine, Todd, and Alex? If they were her friends, they wouldn't choose to hurt her. The same applied to Ben. He claimed to love her, yet all he did was hurt her. She couldn't stay for one more minute in his presence.

"Fine." She shoved the packet of marijuana into her jacket pocket. "You don't want to believe me? That's fine. I've done everything I know to do to prove I've changed—to prove I'm not Kent and I won't keep using drugs. But you don't want to believe me! You'd rather go on thinking the worst, never taking a chance, never admitting that maybe—just maybe—you could be wrong."

Throwing her arms outward, she released a huff. "Okay, don't believe me. Stephanie is right. It isn't my problem, Ben, it's yours. And you're just going to have to deal with it." She spun and headed for the trees.

"Angela!"

Ben's angry voice didn't slow her steps a bit.

"Angela, it's dark! You'll get lost! Come back here!"

"I got myself out here; I'll get myself back!" She didn't even turn around, just forged forward, her hands outstretched as she groped her way through the gray gloom. She heard Ben's muffled voice, but she ignored him and continued her halting progress.

Leaves crunched beneath her tennis shoes, the noise an assault to an otherwise peaceful night. She stomped along, determined to put as much space between herself and Ben as possible. Her chest ached with the desire to cry, but she set her chin and held the hurt inside. He'd made her cry for the last time. No more!

After stumbling noisily forward for several minutes, she paused and listened. No footsteps followed her. Huffing from the effort of moving quickly through the dark, she leaned against a tree for a few moments of rest. She slipped her hands into her pockets, and she encountered the marijuana. The plastic bag crinkled beneath her palm, bringing a rush of memories.

The remembrance of past times—filling her lungs with smoke, experiencing the sensation of floating, being part of a circle of acceptance—brought a flood of desire. Ben already thought she was a user; why not prove him right?

It would be so easy to make a joint. The little squares of paper were scattered all over that area where she'd surprised the boys. She could sneak back there, circle around so Ben wouldn't see. A few draws on a marijuana joint would wash away the pain Ben caused, wash away the feeling of failure, and carry her to a height of pleasure. Her fingers tightened on the packet as a war took place in her heart.

Then she remembered another sensation of floating. Today, on the ropes, gliding from tree to tree while trusting Bruce and Ben to keep her safe. Bruce's words filled her head. *Let God hold you up.* Dropping to her knees on the leaves, Angela lowered her head and poured out her heart to God. She begged Him to remove the desire for drugs once and for all. Then she thanked Him for the opportunity to prove her promise was sincere. Finally, her thoughts turned to Ben.

"God, I don't know what to do about Ben. I love him, but loving him hurts too much. You can take the desire for drugs away. Please take the desire for Ben away, too." She remained on her knees for several more minutes, absorbing the peacefulness of one-on-one time with her heavenly Father. The chill from the ground made her shiver, and she rose clumsily to her feet. Raising her face to the star-studded sky, she whispered a "thank You" for God's endless presence, and then she continued her progress toward camp. Before long, she spotted the glow of the bonfire and heard voices raised in song.

There was one important thing left to do. Her heart pounding, she made her way out of the trees. She glanced over her shoulder. Ben was still back there somewhere. Her heart ached. As much as she still loved him, his actions had proven he would never trust her. Trying to win Ben's approval was a losing battle—one she no longer had the energy to fight.

"Good-bye, Ben," she whispered, then walked slowly to the group gathered around the bonfire. She looked for Robyn and Stephanie and located Stephanie first. She worked her way through the group to Stephanie's side and crouched beside her. Tapping the woman's shoulder, she whispered, "Stephanie? I need to make a phone call. Could you come with me, please?"

Without a word of question, Stephanie rose. The pair walked in silence to the dormitories.

ॐ

Ben made sure the small campfire was completely extinguished before turning back toward the group. His steps felt heavy, labored, and he knew it had nothing to do with the late hour and tiredness from a busy day. The weight of Angela's betrayal wore him down. Once a drug user, always a drug user—isn't that what he'd said? Yet seeing it proved true hurt more than he had imagined. His journey through the trees seemed to take hours—hours of painful reflection.

All of the pleasant images from the day now disappeared, replaced by the sight of Angela standing, shamefaced, with a packet of marijuana in her hand. He shook his head, a feeble attempt to clear the image from his memory, but it remained, permanently imbedded in his mind. And she had taken it with her—stuffed it in her jacket pocket and stormed away.

He replayed that moment of her slipping the marijuana into her pocket over and over. If only he could change the scene. Why hadn't he leaped forward, snatched the packet away from her, and flung it into the fire? Instead, he'd stood there stupidly and let her walk away with it. Which meant Angela was now in possession of marijuana.

Drugs were in violation of camp rules—a cause for immediate dismissal. One word to the campground administrator, and Angela would be sent packing. More importantly, drug possession was a clear violation of her parole. If he contacted her parole officer, her community service would end immediately. She would serve the remainder of her sentence in a detention facility.

His feet scuffed through dried leaves and pine needles as he moved forward, the beam of the flashlight bouncing ahead. He stared at the beam, his thoughts tumbling haphazardly through his confused mind. The remainder of the weekend would be less stressful for him if he didn't have to see her. One word— just one word—and she'd be returned to Petersburg in disgrace. His chest contracted painfully. Could he do that to her even if it meant having the weekend free of her presence? What a price to pay for his own comfort.

And if he told the administrator, Bruce would contact the authorities. Drugs were illegal. Bruce would be obligated to tell. Then Angela wouldn't be at New Beginnings anymore.

That wouldn't necessarily be a bad thing, he told himself. How much easier work would be if he didn't have to see her, be tortured daily by the rush of love and desire that struck with every glimpse of her. Surely if she weren't a part of his everyday routine, he would be able to free himself of the love that had grown for her. Or would he?

The wavering flashlight beam swung back and forth, illuminating the path. His thoughts swung back and forth, illuminating nothing. *Turn her in—it's the right thing to do. Don't turn her in—it's a selfish thing to do.*

He wanted to do the right thing, but the right thing for whom? Turning her in would solve his own problem of having to see her every day. Not turning her in, while giving her a temporary reprieve, would only enable her to continue in drug use.

So turning her in was right for both of them. . .wasn't it?

"Lord, what do I do?" He spoke the words aloud, his anguished thoughts causing his stomach to churn.

Voices and soft laughter drifted through the evening air. He was nearly back to the bonfire. He had to make a decision.

What if he left it to chance? His heart thudded at his own variation of Russian roulette. If he spotted Bruce first, he'd turn Angela over to him. If he spotted Angela first, he'd try to find another way to set things right.

He reached the clearing where people were picking up napkins and crumpled Styrofoam cups, dashing the bonfire with water, and preparing to go back to the dormitories. He scanned the crowd, but he didn't find Angela or Bruce. His heart picked up its tempo. Had she sneaked back to the dorms to make a marijuana cigarette? The smell would certainly alert everyone. He needed to find her, warn her.

That impulse convinced him he didn't want to turn her in. Although he knew it was wrong to keep secret what he'd discovered, a part of him wanted to give Angela one more chance. One more chance to do the right thing. His breath came in spurts out of his nose as he trotted past the groups moving slowly toward the dormitories.

He prepared an ultimatum as he hurried to locate Angela. If she would give him the marijuana, he would dispose of it and keep it secret. But he would make sure she understood if she chose to purchase drugs again, she was on her own. He wouldn't interfere a second time. This would be a one-shot deal. He hoped she'd take it.

As he neared the dorms, beams from a pair of headlights appeared on the lane leading to the campsite. Ben's steps slowed as the car rolled to a stop directly in front of the women's dormitory. His heart skipped a beat when he recognized the insignia on the driver's door. A sheriff's vehicle.

Someone had already discovered Angela had marijuana! So his ultimatum wouldn't be offered after all. Relief and regret mingled in his chest. Though greatly relieved he hadn't had to be the one to make the call, he regretted that it was necessary at all. If only he'd been wrong. If only she hadn't gone looking for drugs tonight. . .

He stopped, watching as the officer turned off the head-lights and stepped out of his vehicle. "Hey, what's going on?" someone behind him asked. The others had caught up and stood in small clusters on the grass outside the dorms.

Ben didn't answer. He wanted no role in Angela's downfall.

The sheriff, standing in the *V* of the open car door, rested his forearm on the top of the vehicle and called, "I'm looking for Angela Fisher."

A mumble of voices sounded behind Ben. His heart twisted in sympathy. How humiliating for her to be summoned this way. He longed to protect her, yet he knew he was powerless. She'd made her choice. Just like Kent, she'd have to suffer the consequences.

The dormitory door opened, throwing a splash of light across the concrete sidewalk. The glint of gold in her tangled curls resembled a halo. "I've never been called an angel," she'd said at supper the night before. Ben's heart ached.

He watched her straighten her shoulders, tossing her gilded curls. "I'm Angela."

eighteen

The sheriff turned toward Angela as the crowd surged forward, curiosity driving them closer to the action. Whispered questions and suppositions floated through the throng, but Ben shut out those voices and concentrated on the sheriff.

Angela met the man halfway between the car and the dormitory. A circle of light from an overhead lantern illuminated the pair, showing the sheriff's stern expression and Angela's pale face. She extended her hands toward him, palms up. Ben held his breath. Did she expect the sheriff to handcuff her? But then he saw that her hands weren't empty. The bag of marijuana rested on her open palms.

"Here you are." Her voice was strong, carrying over the mutters behind him.

Another flurry of voices broke out.

"What is it?"

"I think it's some sort of drug."

"Where would she have gotten that?"

Ben took a step forward, an attempt to block the voices behind him. He needed to hear the sheriff and Angela.

The sheriff took the packet and turned it over in his hands, a scowl pinching his eyebrows. "Well, you were right. It certainly appears to be marijuana."

Ben's jaw nearly dropped. Based on the sheriff's words, Angela must have alerted him herself. But she wouldn't have done that if—

The sheriff continued. "Is this all of it?"

Angela's shoulder lifted in a slight shrug. "I don't know if there was more. This is all they dropped."

"Dropped?"

"Yes, sir. When the boys ran off, they left this behind. I just picked it up."

The sheriff reached into his breast pocket and removed a small pad and pencil. He flipped the pad open and looked at Angela. "How did you happen to join these boys?" The sheriff's sharp tone made Ben cringe, but Angela straightened her shoulders and faced the man squarely.

"I was taking a walk, doing some thinking. I had no idea anyone else was out there when I started my walk. I heard laughter and saw a fire. I was curious, so I approached them. It was just. . .coincidence."

"So you had no intention of using the drugs?"

Angela's gaze flitted briefly to the listening crowd. Her face looked pale, yet there was a calmness in her eyes that spoke of strength. "To be honest, sir, when I saw what they had, I was tempted. There was a time when I found a release in drugs. But I'm not that person anymore. I made a promise to God that I would never use drugs again. I intend to keep that promise."

The sheriff gave a brusque nod. "And you don't know who these boys are?"

"No. This is my first time at Camp Fellowship. I'm from Petersburg, and I don't know any of the local families." Her face crunched for a moment, her head tipping to spill curls across her shoulder. "I got the impression from their behavior, though, that the boys had been at that location before. They seemed familiar with the area."

Ben felt his heart beat in his temples. Thinking of the

campfire he'd extinguished, he realized Angela was right. The amount of ashes within the circle of rocks, and the scattering of old cans and bottles in the little clearing, indicated more than one party had taken place out there.

"Could you find the clearing again, if need be?"

"Yes, sir. I believe so."

Ben nodded. He could help.

"Do you suppose you could give a description of the boys?" the sheriff asked.

Angela's face pinched into a thoughtful frown. "It was pretty dark, but I think I could. It might not be very accurate, though."

The swell of voices behind Ben started again, covering the descriptions Angela provided while the sheriff wrote on the notepad. The sheriff finished his scribbling then looked at Angela again. "While I appreciate you calling this in, your past history does give me reason to question your lack of involvement."

Angela nodded, her head low. Ben's heart ached at the dejected, shame-filled pose. It ached more when he realized he'd treated her just as the sheriff was now.

The sheriff asked, "Were any other campers around who could substantiate your story?"

Without a second thought, Ben stepped forward. "Sir." He waited until the sheriff looked at him. Angela didn't move. "I was out there, too."

The sheriff angled his pen against the pad. "You are?"

"Ben Atchison." Ben stated his address and telephone.

"And you were at the scene?"

Ben clarified, "Not at first. Angela went out on her own. But when she didn't come back to the bonfire, I got worried.

I thought maybe she'd lost her way in the dark, so I went looking for her. Before I came upon the clearing, I very clearly heard her telling someone to give her the marijuana."

He looked at Angela, wishing she would meet his gaze, but she remained silent with her eyes downcast. He went on. "She didn't ask to use it; she just told them to hand it over. When I reached the clearing, I saw the three boys run off into the woods. They dropped the marijuana before they left."

The sheriff wrote a little more then flipped the pad closed and slipped it into his breast pocket. "Thank you, Mr. Atchison." Turning back to Angela, he said, "Miss Fisher, I will contact your parole office to let him know what transpired this evening. He may need to ask you a few questions when you return to Petersburg."

Angela finally lifted her head and offered a small nod in reply.

For the first time, the sheriff lost his stern expression. "I'm sure this was a difficult decision for you, to call me, knowing the possible repercussions. I appreciate your making the call. Obviously, we don't want our local youth involved in drug use. Hopefully we'll be able to identify these boys and get them some help."

"I hope so, sir." Her voice sounded weak, its former firm tone wilting.

The sheriff strode to his vehicle and drove away from the camp while several people pushed forward, surrounding Angela. Their words of praise for her actions filled Ben's ears. After a few minutes of excited activity, they began to wander into the dormitories, leaving only Angela, Stephanie, and Robyn waiting under the light of the lantern. When Angela's gaze shifted to meet Ben's, Stephanie and Robyn exchanged a look behind Angela's head.

Stephanie said, "We'll turn in now, Angela."

"Yes, but holler if you need anything," Robyn said, shooting a brief glance in Ben's direction.

He hung his head. The women had cause for concern, based on his past behavior. He hoped he could rectify that now. He waited until Robyn and Stephanie shut the dormitory door behind them before whispering a simple question.

"Need a hug?"

❧

Angela gave a start. Had she heard him correctly? The tender look on his face proved she hadn't misunderstood. And a hug was exactly what she needed.

She took one hesitant step toward him, and he closed the gap with three firm strides. She flung herself into Ben's embrace. His arms closed around her, holding her securely against his chest, and she pressed her cheek to his collarbone as tears stung behind her eyes. How she'd needed this hug! And to have it come from Ben. . . She thought her heart might burst from the emotion that pressed upward.

She allowed the warmth of Ben's arms and his heartbeat beneath her ear to soothe away every worry of the last several minutes. How she'd feared the sheriff would refuse to listen to her explanation, would simply haul her away in disgrace. Her knees still quivered slightly as the tension slowly drained away. She replayed words of congratulations and approval from the other campers at her courage, but as much as she appreciated the support of the others, what she really needed to know is what Ben thought of her now.

Reluctantly, she pulled away. His hands slipped from her waist as she took a step backward and lifted her face to meet his gaze. "Thank you for the hug, Ben. I—I needed it."

His sweet smile—the smile she'd longed to see for so long—made her knees go weak again. But not from anxiety.

"You're welcome."

She swallowed the lump that formed in her throat. "Could—could we talk?"

"I think we should." Ben stretched out his hand, pressing his palm to the small of her back. A tingle traveled from her spine to her hairline, prickling her scalp. Without a word, he guided her across the shadowed landscape to the bench in the middle of the courtyard. They sat, one at each end of the bench, with a gap between them. Angling her knees toward the center, she faced Ben.

The overhead tree branches waving in front of the lantern cast speckled shadows across Ben's face, but she could make out his expression. None of the recrimination of previous days remained. Her heart thudded in a hopeful double beat.

"Ben, I want you to know that everything I told the sheriff was true. I didn't go out to that clearing to make a drug deal. I just happened upon those boys, and I tried to take the marijuana away from them so they wouldn't use it. And when I told him I never intend to use drugs again, I meant that, too."

He opened his mouth, but she held up her hand, stilling his words. She had to be completely honest with him. She wanted no secrets between them to create problems in the future—if they were to have a future.

"Out there, alone in the trees, I thought about opening up that marijuana and rolling a joint. It would have been so easy. No one was around, and I knew from past experience the marijuana would give me a few minutes of escape. My heart was aching, and a part of me really wanted that escape."

She kept her gaze pinned to his, determined to tell all. "But something stopped me. I realized I no longer wanted drugs to be my support system, my escape. I only wanted God. I asked Him to help me resist the desire for drugs, and He answered, Ben. He took the desire away. I know I won't ever do drugs again. The need for them is gone. I have all I need in my relationship with Him."

For long seconds they sat together. Only the gentle lullaby of dry leaves rattled in the evening breeze. Ben's gaze didn't waver from hers, and none of the reproach she'd seen before flashed through his eyes. Gathering her courage, she went on. "There's one more thing I need to say." She paused, drew a deep breath, and released it slowly. Looking directly into his dark eyes, she said, "I love you, Ben. And I know you love me."

The muscles in his jaw clenched, and his Adam's apple bobbed in a swallow. "How do you know that?" His voice sounded husky.

"You told me yesterday when you said you couldn't watch someone else you loved walk the path of drug addiction. So I know you love me." Leaning forward, she placed her trembling hand on his knee. "But, Ben, loving me isn't enough. You have to be able to trust me, too. Love and trust go hand in hand, and if one is missing, there can never be unity."

Pausing, she took another slow breath to bring her erratic heartbeat under control. She feared the answer to the next question, yet she had to ask it. "Do—do you think you can ever learn to trust me when I say I won't use drugs again?"

Ben turned his face to peer across the grounds. A pulse in his temple spoke of his inner battle. Angela held her breath, waiting, praying. Finally he brought his gaze around to meet hers.

Placing his hand over hers, he linked fingers with her. "Angela, what you did tonight took so much courage. Calling the sheriff, telling him you had marijuana in your possession. . . When I think of what could have happened to you. . . You could have been picked up and taken to jail without being given a chance to explain. Yet you took the chance because you knew you were innocent."

Tears glinted in his eyes. "I'm so proud of you. And your actions proved to me your honesty when you say you won't use drugs again."

Angela released the breath she'd been holding in a whoosh of relief. She nearly melted, and Ben's arms stretched out, capturing her and drawing her across the bench to hold her snugly beneath his chin. Cradling her in his arms, he went on in a tear-choked voice.

"I'm so sorry I doubted you. I let what happened to Kent put blinders on my eyes. I've watched you over the past weeks, and I've seen so much evidence of growth. That verse in Ephesians, the one about being blameless and holy in His sight?"

She offered a slight nod, cuddling closer, secure within the circle of his arms.

"That's what you are, Angela—holy. Jesus washed your heart clean when you invited Him in. He sees you as holy, yet I refused to see it. Instead, I deliberately focused on your past. My fear of being hurt again built a wall around you that wouldn't allow you to shine. I know I hurt you with my harsh words and judgmental attitude."

Pulling back slightly, he cupped her chin and lifted her face so he could look directly into her eyes. "Can you forgive me?"

Angela smiled, her lips quivering as she battled tears. "Of

course I forgive you." Saying the words brought a rush of relief so great, Angela wilted against his chest once more.

His lips touched the crown of her head. "Thank you."

Still nestling, Angela shared a private thought. "When I first met Kent, and I found out his disability was the result of drug use, I felt so. . .grateful."

Ben's hands rubbed up and down her back. "Grateful?" His breath stirred her hair.

"Yes. That could have been me, if I hadn't gotten caught. He reminds me of where I might be if I hadn't allowed God into my life. When I've been tempted to go back to drugs, I've thought of Kent, of how his life has changed because of his choices, and it's helped me choose more wisely."

"Oh, Angela. . ." The words came out in a sigh, and she felt his hands still as he pressed his lips to the top of her head.

Shifting slightly, she looked up at him. "Are you offended?"

"Offended?" He smiled, but she saw a glimmer of tears in his eyes. "No, my sweet Angela. You've given me hope that Kent's life isn't wasted. He still has a purpose. God used him to help you choose to stay clean." He shook his head, still smiling. "Thank you for telling me that."

She snuggled again, her eyes closed, breathing deeply to inhale the scents of the moment—damp earth, dry leaves, and the musky scent of Ben's skin. It was a potpourri she wanted to remember forever.

When Ben spoke again, the rumble of his deep voice vibrated beneath Angela's ear. "You've shared with me. Now let me share with you." Taking hold of her shoulders, he gently pulled her from her nestling spot. His fingers caressed her upper arms as he gazed into her face.

"You said love and trust go hand in hand. You're right. I've loved you for weeks, yet I withheld my trust. But no more. I promise you, Angela, from this moment forward, I will never again question your honesty. I will see you as Jesus sees you, as a new creature, holy and blameless in His sight."

His features swam as tears filled her eyes, and she blinked, swallowing as happy sobs pressed for release.

"He has cast your mistakes far away, and I promise I will not allow those past mistakes to impact the way I view you today. You are beautiful, Angela. Beautiful, pure, and holy. I love you, and I trust you."

She felt the spill of warm tears down her cheeks, but instead of reaching to brush them away, she reached for Ben. He captured her in his arms, drawing her near once more. His lips met hers, warm and tender.

Laughter rang from within her—joy-filled and healing. "Oh, Ben, I love you so much."

Cupping her cheeks, he pressed his forehead to hers. His whisper melted her heart. "Do you believe me? Do you trust me to keep my promise?"

"Oh, yes. No broken promises. Not ever."

Ben sealed the promise with another kiss.

epilogue

Ben gave Kent's bow tie a quick tug, straightening it beneath his cousin's chin. With a smile, he said, "Wow, you look pretty spiffy there, cuz."

Kent's smile lit his face. "I am. . .best man."

Ben chuckled. "That you are, Kent. That you are." When they were fifteen, the year before their fathers' deaths, the boys had made a pact to stand up for one another when they married. It pleased Ben that, despite Kent's challenges, the promise was being kept.

The glow in Kent's eyes convinced Ben his cousin understood the significance of the event. And, thankfully, over the past three months, Kent's relationship with Angela had developed into a warm friendship. No jealousy lurked in Kent's eyes, only pleasure in his role in the wedding. It was an answer to prayer.

Ben walked to the mirror hanging near the door of the small room where he and the groomsmen readied themselves for the ceremony. Looking at his reflection, he had to smile. When he'd first spotted Angela at New Beginnings, would he have imagined meeting her at the head of an aisle while dressed in a black tuxedo and turquoise bow tie? Not in a million years. . .

Unlikely, he decided. That's what it was. Unlikely. Unlikely that he could fall in love with a former drug-abusing rich girl who didn't even know how to cook. Unlikely that a woman uncomfortable around those with disabilities would fall in love with a man whose life's call was to work with disabled adults.

Even though Angela was the opposite of what he had thought he was looking for in a wife, the love in his heart was so strong and so right. Unlikely didn't matter a bit when it came to God's will. They were perfect for each other. He knew that from the depth of his heart.

Eagerness built to go to the sanctuary, to fill his senses with the image of his bride coming down the aisle. Keeping with tradition, she had adamantly refused to allow him so much as a peek this morning.

"It's bad luck!" she had insisted last night after the rehearsal.

"But wouldn't it be good to take pictures before the ceremony?" It made sense to him to get all the picture snapping out of the way ahead of time.

But she had shaken her head, making her curls bounce. "No, Ben." Stepping into his embrace, she had peered up at him with serious eyes. "I want our first look at one another tomorrow to be in our wedding finery. I want to cherish your expression when you see how I've tried to please you with my appearance."

He had chuckled softly, certain she could come marching down that aisle in a pair of worn-out blue jeans and holey T-shirt and it wouldn't change how he felt about her. But instead of voicing that thought, he'd promised, "Okay. No peeks before the ceremony." Then he'd tapped the end of her nose and teased, "But it'd better be worth it."

She had tipped up on her toes to give him a quick smack on the lips. "Oh, I promise. It'll be worth it."

He smiled again, imagining her in the room next door,

primping, teasing her curls into place, adjusting her gown. . .
His stomach clenched. How much longer would he have to
wait?

Spinning from the mirror, he glanced at his wristwatch—
his wedding gift from Angela's parents—and heaved a sigh of
relief. It was time. He marched over to Kent and took hold of
the handles on his wheelchair. "Ready to go?"

"Yes. Let's. . .get married."

Ben laughed. "You got it."

⁂

Angela sent a quick glance down the length of her gown of
snowy white. Seed pearls and sequins formed delicate swirls on
the unblemished backdrop of satin. She touched the beaded
band at her throat and felt her pulse racing.

Turning to her father, she whispered, "Is my hair okay?
Everything still intact?"

He pulled down his brows, seeming to examine the elaborate
twist held in place with pearled pins. She had deliberately
pulled a few stands free to fall in spiraling curls along her neck
and cheek. Her father tugged one of those free curls, smiling
as it sprang back into place. "It looks okay to me." Then his
lips tipped into a smile. "You look beautiful, Angela. Simply
radiant."

"Oh, Daddy. . ." If everything went wrong during the wedding ceremony, her father's words were enough to make up
for it.

The lilting melody of Bach's Arioso drifted from the sanctuary,
and Angela sucked in a breath of eagerness. She whispered,
"Daddy! It's time!"

His fingers tightened on her arm, his smile warm. "Are you
sure you want to go through with it?"

"Daddy, please!" She giggled, pulling at his arm. Her father had asked her that question at least four times already, but she wasn't offended. For the first time in her life, her father was taking a genuine interest in her. Even though she had insisted on being married in unpretentious Grace Chapel instead of the huge church downtown, even though she had chosen a man of moderate means instead of a man of wealth, even though she had chosen a simple ceremony followed by cake and punch rather than a grandiose celebration, her parents had agreed and supported her. She and Ben had every confidence that eventually their witness, combined with Aunt Eileen's, would win her parents to the Lord. Angela had never been happier.

"Okay," her father chuckled. "Let's go."

They stepped through the door as the guests rose in honor of the bride. Ben was hidden from view until Angela turned the corner at the foot of the center aisle, but when she got her first glimpse of her groom, she released a gasp of pleasure.

Oh, Father-God, thank You for the gift of this man. The sparkle of joy in Ben's deep blue eyes drew Angela like a magnet, and she sped her steps instead of staying in time with the gentle flow of music. She read in his eyes a silent message: *You were worth this wait.*

She answered with a smile of her own: *You're everything I've dreamed of.*

Facing the minister, Ben's warm palm on her spine, Angela drank in the message based on First Corinthians 13. When the minister read, " 'Love believes all things. . .' " she felt Ben's fingers press against her flesh. She flicked a brief glance at him, assuring him she made the same promise.

When she spoke her vows, her voice catching as emotion

filled her throat, she offered a silent prayer to God to honor Him by keeping every pledge made to Ben on this day.

Tears coursed down her cheeks when she was finally able to lift her face to receive her first kiss as Mrs. Ben Atchison. Ben cupped her cheeks, his thumbs along her jaw. She clasped the backs of his hands and smiled through her tears.

She whispered as the guests broke into applause, "To God be all praise and honor."

"Amen," Ben whispered in reply. His lips captured hers once more, delivering a promise of wonderful things to come.

A Letter To Our Readers

Dear Reader:
In order that we might better contribute to your reading
enjoyment, we would appreciate your taking a few minutes
to respond to the following questions. We welcome your
comments and read each form and letter we receive. When
completed, please return to the following:

Fiction Editor
Heartsong Presents
PO Box 719
Uhrichsville, Ohio 44683

1. Did you enjoy reading *Promising Angela* by Kim Vogel Sawyer?
   ❏ Very much! I would like to see more books by this author!
   ❏ Moderately. I would have enjoyed it more if

   _____

   _____

   _____

2. Are you a member of **Heartsong Presents**? ❏ Yes ❏ No
   If no, where did you purchase this book? _____

   _____

3. How would you rate, on a scale from 1 (poor) to 5 (superior),
   the cover design? _____

4. On a scale from 1 (poor) to 10 (superior), please rate the
   following elements.

   ____ Heroine   ____ Plot
   ____ Hero   ____ Inspirational theme
   ____ Setting   ____ Secondary characters

5. These characters were special because? _____
_____
_____

6. How has this book inspired your life? _____
_____
_____

7. What settings would you like to see covered in future
   Heartsong Presents books? _____
_____
_____

8. What are some inspirational themes you would like to see
   treated in future books? _____
_____
_____

9. Would you be interested in reading other **Heartsong
   Presents** titles? ❑ Yes   ❑ No

10. Please check your age range:
    ❑ Under 18   ❑ 18-24
    ❑ 25-34   ❑ 35-45
    ❑ 46-55   ❑ Over 55

Name _____
Occupation _____
Address _____
City, State, Zip _____